Crime turns up in ingenious variety to celebrate the 25th anniversary of Lt. Luis Mendoza's first appearance on the mystery scene.

Beset by two insistent puzzlers—how to nail the pair efficiently heisting the best restaurants in town and to find some clue to the brutal murderer of the elderly, well-to-do widow—Mendoza and his hard-pressed colleagues somehow cope with a host of other crimes crowding the blotter.

Meanwhile, Luis continues his education in domesticity by Alison and the twins, Higgins basks in new fatherhood, Hackett wages his eternal war with the bathroom scales, and Landers seesaws between hope and despair in pursuit of his girl.

In short, the 25th Mendoza is one not to be missed.

Deuces Wild

DELL SHANNON

Deuces Wild

William Morrow & Company, Inc.
New York   1975

Printed in the United States of America.

1 2 3 4 5 79 78 77 76 75

Library of Congress Cataloging in Publication Data

Linington, Elizabeth.
  Deuces wild.

  I. Title.
PZ4.L756Di [PS3562.I515]   813'.5'4   74-20815
ISBN 0-688-00335-4

Book design by Helen Roberts

". . . Their oppression stems from their failure to mature into adults. They are, in the last analysis, a miserably undisciplined generation, lacking patience and routine perseverance: seeking instant solutions to stubborn problems. To the extent that the kids cannot marshal their inner resources and direct them toward achievement, they naturally feel oppressed . . . but do not discern the nature of that oppression. Their literature and art express the weakness. Their literature is childish, garish, and undisciplined. Their music is unstructured and simple and noisy. . . . Their lack of morals is in itself an oppressive facet of their lives. Somewhere within them they know there must be boundaries on human conduct. You do not routinely murder thy neighbor . . .

". . . Too many of the kids have a compact with the devil."

—RICHARD WHEELER
The Children of Darkness

Deuces Wild

One

Mendoza was going to be late, and for once he didn't care. He added cream to a third cup of coffee and lit another cigarette. "Why I don't resign the thankless job," he said bitterly, "I don't know. All the slogging labor we expend in catching them, and then the Goddamned courts— We'll never get anybody for Dagostino, there's no handle. And that damn judge yesterday—"

"You wouldn't know what to do with yourself," said Alison automatically. She was drying the dishes as Mrs. MacTaggart washed them, briskly putting them away; she looked efficient and boyish with her red hair swathed in a terry turban. "Now where are those two?—honestly, take your eyes off them a minute and—if they're over the fence again—" She peered out the window over the sink.

"Ah, it's a while since they took that notion," said Mrs. MacTaggart, but she hung away her dish towel and went to open the back door. Three of the cats—Bast, Sheba and Nefertite—were sunning themselves on the back porch; of El Señor the wicked there was no sign; and

-9

the Old English sheepdog Cedric had disinterred a bone and was thoughtfully chewing it in the middle of the yard. In a moment the twins appeared from behind the garage, arguing vehemently about something.

"And ten to one," said Mendoza, "something new went down overnight to make us more thankless work. With two men off— ¡Dios! Why did I ever want to be a cop?"

The twins erupted through the back door. "Mama!" said Terry tearfully. "Look! All dirty! Want a nice clean dress!" She exhibited a minute stain of mud on her white pinafore.

"Heavens above," said Alison. "I suppose if one of them had to inherit your fanatic persnickitiness, it's just as well it should be the girl. Look, Terry, it'll brush right off, see?"

"Want an *all* clean dress!" demanded Terry.

"She's a silly," said Johnny. "*¡Estúpido!*" At nearly four, the twins were developing into definite personalities.

"I am not *estúpido!* Don't like to be all dirty! Mama—"

"Now, my lamb," said Mrs. MacTaggart, "we'll just sponge it off and it'll not show at all."

"*I* can see where it was," said Terry.

"Exactly like your father," said Alison.

"And what else would you expect?" retorted Mendoza, getting up reluctantly and automatically straightening his tie, yanking down his cuffs. As usual he was immaculate in silver-gray Italian silk, snowy shirt and discreet dark tie, his hairline moustache neatly trimmed. "I feel like taking the day off. Going for a nice long drive up the coast, or—or renting a yacht or something. I'm tired of reading autopsy reports. I might run over to Vegas and find a hot poker game."

"For goodness' sake, go!" said Alison. "Wherever. It's

after nine and Mairí and I want to get at those curtains —now we're all behind, we'll never finish the dining room today—"

"Ah, once we get at it it won't take long, *achara*."

"Shoo," said Alison firmly. "Go and read autopsy reports, Luis."

"The happy home," said Mendoza, but he found his hat and went out the back door. El Señor was stalking a bird at the end of the yard; he wouldn't catch it—he never caught anything—so Mendoza didn't go to the rescue. He backed the Ferrari out to the top of the circular drive, reflecting that it was the wrong time of year to have spring fever; a hot sunny Friday in August, the air still and stagnant. But, as usual with summer across southern California, the case load at Robbery-Homicide, LAPD, was a little heavier than usual, and Mendoza was tired of it. He was tired of the monotony of random violence and death, the stupid people, the old round of crime these days more violent and bloody and wanton. He'd been dealing with it for nearly twenty-five years on the thankless job, and rather often he felt very tired of it.

But they were shorthanded at the office; he'd better go in. He caught the light at the corner of Hollywood Boulevard and Laurel Canyon, and shoved in the cigarette lighter as he waited, his mind sliding over the cases they had on hand at the moment.

The Dagostino thing was dead; there was nowhere to go on it. Just an old man beaten and robbed on the street; they didn't even know how much he'd had on him. It had probably been—as it all too often was these days— one or more punks looking for loot to support the habit. There were, as usual, unidentified bodies waiting at the morgue. Male teenager dead of an overdose; female ditto; elderly man dead of a heart attack; and a hit-run victim— the first three run of the mill, but it was a little funny that the hit-run one hadn't been identified: an ordinary-looking middle-aged woman, good clothes, forty bucks in a coin purse; she hadn't been a derelict. To be hoped she'd get identified sometime. There had been a gang rumble last week, one dead of knife wounds, and six of those punks would be coming up for arraignment next week. There had been, on the Central beat which was Mendoza's beat, nine heist-jobs in the last ten days, and they still had victims coming in to look at mug shots and were still pulling in men with the right sort of records to question, without having got anything definite yet. Then on Wednesday they had a new body—not just the casual body, but an apparent Murder One: female found in MacArthur Park. Palliser had been on that, said it looked like strangulation; there'd probably be an autopsy report sometime today. And the situation never stayed static: there would doubtless be other business coming along for Robbery-Homicide.

They were three men short. Detectives Shogart and Henry Glasser were off on vacation, though Glasser would be back on Monday; when Detective Tom Landers might be back was debatable. Landers and his policewoman, Phil O'Neill, had got engaged in June; ten days ago, with the support of several colleagues as witnesses, they had got themselves officially married and taken off on a honeymoon. Both of them having some legitimate leave saved up, they might be gone some time.

When Mendoza came into the office he found both his senior sergeants there, chatting with Sergeant Lake who was manning the switchboard. "You've both got spring fever too?" he said. "I nearly didn't come in. Don't tell me something new's gone down."

"When doesn't it?" said Higgins reasonably. "Another heist on the street last night—Conway left a report. Couple of girls who work for the phone company, on their way home—held up in the parking lot and knocked around a little. I'd deduce, a couple of punks with the habit. No descriptions, of course. I just got back from the hospital."

"I see," said Hackett, sounding resigned, "that you wasted your time in court yesterday." They both followed Mendoza into his office.

"¡Mil rayos!" said Mendoza, flinging himself down in his desk chair and reaching for the lighter. "Don't mention the punks to me, Arturo! That Gebhart—mainlining H and ending up killing a man, and that Goddamned judge takes a reduced plea of manslaughter and hands him a one to three! Will you take a bet he doesn't kill somebody else before the dope gets him? Or that his lawyer gets him out on parole after he's served three months?"

"I will not," said Hackett with a grimace. "You haven't seen the paper this morning, I take it." He and Higgins together dwarfed Mendoza's office; Mendoza looked up from one to the other suspiciously.

"¿Qué? Now what?"

"Maybe they were a little short of news," said Hackett. "Anyway, they covered the Gebhart hearing, er, lavishly—"

"That stepmother of his used to be a star on Broadway," said Higgins through a yawn.

"And?" Mendoza took the *Times* from Hackett and ran his eye down the lefthand column, under the headline *Reduced Pleas For Accused Killer.* "Oh, for God's sake. Well, it's no secret. But— ¿Y eso qué importa?" He shrugged, but reread the paragraph. As he said, no secret, but as it happened this was the first time it had got into the papers.

"Testifying for the prosecution, veteran officer Lieutenant Luis Mendoza was reprimanded twice by Judge Ernest Becker as he crossed verbal swords with defense attorney Gilman. Lieutenant Mendoza, 'the Millionaire

Cop,' expensively tailored and obviously annoyed at the lesser charge finally accepted by the court, exchanged angry words with Mr. Gilman during the hearing. Rumor has it—"

"*¡Disparate!*" said Mendoza. "Rumor! I stay on the job, despite all my ill-gained gold, because I like to persecute these poor oppressed victims of society! If you want my opinion, Art, Gilman envies my tailoring. He'd like to be called dapper too, but he has a deplorable taste in ties." He pushed the paper aside. "I knew there'd be an autopsy report. That female—"

"We may have her identified," said Higgins. "Woman came in half an hour ago—John took her down to the morgue. Art and I just left a couple down in R. and I. looking at mug shots, I suppose we'd better check back on them."

"And they won't recognize any," said Mendoza. But his eyes strayed back to the *Times* and he frowned.

"I hope Matt remembered to cover that arraignment," said Hackett suddenly. "Webley."

"I reminded him." Higgins yawned again.

"That's a funny one, you know, George? I thought when we heard it, one of the queerest damned·things we've ever had. Makes you believe in predestination. I went to this literary tea once—"

"*¡Maravilloso!*" muttered Mendoza, and Higgins laughed.

"No, but it just came back to me," pursued Hackett seriously. "Angel took me. This woman who writes mysteries, and Angel likes her stuff, she gave a talk—and one thing stuck in my mind, because it shows how different books are from real life. She said in fiction you can't have anything happen by coincidence. Well, my God, we're always running into coincidences on the job. But this Web-

14

ley, now that's a case where it seems to me coincidence was more like fate. Here he's covered all his tracks, got a new identity and job and background, not one damn thing anywhere to tie him to that murdered wife back in New Jersey—and it just happens that her best friend takes a trip to California and sits at the next table to him at the Brown Derby. Talk about fate—"

"I just hope Matt covered it," said Mendoza. He started to read the autopsy report. As Hackett and Higgins started out, Sergeant John Palliser came in.

"N.G.," he reported briefly. "She didn't know her. I didn't think she would—her daughter's been on the missing list over a year and Carey thinks she just took off with a bunch of drifters. Might be in a commune back in Massachusetts, or anywhere. So this one's still Jane Doe." He lit a cigarette. "No snapshots, George?"

Higgins grinned amiably. These days he'd got used to having his firsthand family, Margaret Emily being eleven months old now. "You're the one ought to be passing snapshots around."

"I never could work a camera," said Palliser, who had just turned into a father last March. "And having suffered through all the snapshots from you and Jase this last year—"

"Where is Jase, by the way?" asked Hackett. "I haven't laid eyes on him this morning."

"Oh, there was a call came in just after you went downstairs," said Palliser casually. "New body, somewhere on the Hollywood freeway."

"¿Qué es esto?" said Mendoza. "And they say women's work—" The autopsy report wasn't much help on Jane Doe. An ordinary-sized Caucasian female between twenty and twenty-five, blonde, had borne at least one child: dental chart enclosed; death caused by manual strangulation probably after midnight last Tuesday night; no evidence of sexual molestation.

Hackett and Higgins wandered out, and Sergeant Lake came in with a telex sheet. "NCIC," he said briefly. "A hell of a thing, but what they expect us to do with this I don't know."

Mendoza abandoned the autopsy report and took the telex. "*¡Porvida!*" he said after glancing at it, and handed it to Palliser. "Just what the hell Merced thinks we can do about it—"

Merced was three hundred and some miles upstate, in the inland valley: not a big town, probably a quiet town as a rule; but it had just had a spectacular multiple murder. An entire family of six, parents, two teenage girls, two younger children, shot and stabbed and stuffed into closets, the house ransacked. By the medical report, last Sunday or Monday night, the bodies only found on Tuesday when relatives got worried enough to investigate. From various witnesses the Merced police had now heard that the teenage girls had recently made some new friends at a local kids' hangout, and the parents had objected to them. The new friends were not local: by what witnesses could say, two couples of drifters—the expectable appurtenances, backpacks, scruffy clothes, the long hair, one of the males sporting a beard; they had a beat-up old jalopy, and had boasted of making rock-festivals all across the country. Merced thought L.A. would like to know about them because two witnesses had stated that the license-plate frame on the old jalopy bore the legend *Bob Hauger Ford Los Angeles*. The car might be a Ford about ten years old, white or blue, a sedan.

"Go and ask," said Palliser, riffling through the yellow pages. "Bob Hauger Ford, here it is, out on La Cienega. I seem to recall it's been there some time, hardly a new agency. But there'll be a used lot, and how many cars with the same plate frame around? We can ask, but it's an empty gesture." He drifted out.

Five minutes later Jason Grace came in. "So you finally decided to come to work."

"*Vaya el diablo*," said Mendoza amiably. "I heard there's a new body."

Grace sat down and brought out a cigarette. If his light gray suit wasn't personally tailored, he was as dapper as Mendoza, his clipped moustache as neat; his chocolate brown face wore a meditative look.

"Something a little offbeat. What am I saying, damned offbeat. We've got five witnesses coming in. People in a car pool—they were right behind this heap, it's either a Ford or a Chevy about six years old, either black or dark blue, no make on the plate, of course—"

"They have eyes and see not."

"—And they all say it was doing about thirty-five in the right lane of the Hollywood freeway when this girl was shoved out of the front seat. Their car just missed ramming the Ford or Chevy or whatever when it stopped—driver hit the brake hard. He started to get out—the only thing they agree on is it was a he—and then changed his mind and took off like a scared jackrabbit—I quote one of the witnesses. And when they looked, the girl had gone over the guardrail down onto the Pasadena freeway. A hundred and fifty feet at a guess—"

"And isn't that offbeat indeed," said Mendoza. "D.O.A.?"

"But very," said Grace. "No I.D. If you want an educated guess, she was one of these kids hitchhiking around the country. Pick up with anybody, ones like her or anybody offered a ride. Her backpack went over with her. I fetched it in. The usual assortment—a few clothes, a little costume jewelry, cheap camera, deck of Tarot cards—*nada más*."

"God give me patience," said Mendoza the longtime agnostic. "Another Jane Doe. These stupid kids doing their own thing—no morals or manners or common sense in a carload!"

Grace said philosophically, "They're still the minority. But it does seem these days they're the ones giving us a lot of work, all right. I suppose, if you want to be fatalistic about it—"

"Fate!" said Mendoza. "Art and his coincidences—my God, why I didn't quit this job when the old man died and all the loot showed up—"

"Oh, yes," said Grace amusedly, "I saw you made the *Times* this morning."

Sergeant Lake came in with another telex from the National Crime Information Center. It was of academic interest only. There had been a job pulled in Sacramento last week, the newest switch on the bank-heist, bank manager's wife held hostage for ransom. Prints lifted at the house had given Sacramento the name of a con with a little record on P.A. from Leavenworth; he had just been picked up over in Oregon. There had been at least two other men on the job; possibly he would now tell Sacramento who they were.

Landers' Corvair had seen its best days and needed some work, so they had taken Phil's practically new bright green Gremlin. They were both dedicated LAPD officers (though as Phil said, if her mother had known she'd grow up to be a police officer she could have chosen something more suitable than Phillippa Rosemary) but right now they were also reasonably young and in love, and they both had some time saved up. It didn't much matter when they got back, in reasonable limits.

They had wandered up the coast ("We'll stop and see your family on the way back," said Phil) and found an old comfortable motel off the beaten track north of Santa

Rosa; there was an isolated beach a mile away, and they stayed.

"But we'll have to stop and see Sue," said Phil lazily. "Family is family after all, Tom."

Landers regarded her small and satisfactory person fondly, where she was stretched out on the beach towel beside him, her new tan complimentary to her white bathing suit and flaxen curls. "I suppose." Her sister lived in San Francisco. "And cut down inland to Fresno." That was where his family lived. "We don't have to stay more than a couple of days."

"And I suppose we ought to be back by the end of the month," said Phil regretfully.

In a quiet suburb of the city of Stockton, that late Friday afternoon, a nearly new Buick pulled up in front of a comfortable old two-story house. As the driver got out, the big black dog eagerly following him, the house door opened and a stocky middle-aged man hurried out in welcome.

"See you got here all right, boy! Good trip?"

"Once I got out of the L.A. traffic." They clasped hands affectionately. "It's good to see you, John. How's the family?"

"Fine—Mamie's been fussing over dinner for you all afternoon, and Bob's all set up at the idea of his first hunting trip. Well, you can't call it that in August—"

"Get a few rabbits maybe," said the other man with a laugh. "Just the idea of getting out in the open air—away from the rat race a week or so at least."

"Christine O.K.? That's good." The other man patted the dog as she pressed against his legs. "Good girl, Bess— bet you're glad to be out of the city too, hah? I thought we might go up beyond Pinecrest, set up camp along the stream. Maybe get some decent fishing."

"Fine—that's pretty country up there."

"You sound a mite fed up with L.A., Fred—new job not going so good?" They started for the house, bearing the one suitcase and long gun-case between them.

"No, no, the job's fine—means a good deal more money too, but it's good to get away for a while."

As they went in, a plump smiling matron came to kiss the visitor warmly. "You look as if you could do with some vacation, Fred—and goodness knows I'll be glad to get the men out from under my feet for a week. Come in, come in—dinner's nearly ready. Bob! Here's your Uncle Fred! And I suppose this blessed dog's starving too—"

"Starving to put up some rabbits in open country again! How'd the pups turn out, Fred?"

"Six good ones. Ritter bought two he picked out as show possibles—"

"Oh, bench!"

"But we sold the rest to that field kennel in Arizona— Well, Bob! My God, you've grown a foot since last year!"

The gangling teenager laughed excitedly. "You look great, Uncle Fred—how's Aunt Christine? Dad says we'll leave real early tomorrow, get up there to make camp by noon—gee, it's going to be great!"

"Let's get your bag upstairs. Fred, while Mamie puts dinner on."

In the rather bare but comfortable bedroom upstairs, Fred said, "It's good to see Bob's turned out such a normal good kid. Some of the teenagers you see these days—God, it makes you wonder—"

"It sure as hell does. But I don't worry about Bob— he's all right."

At nine-thirty that Friday night Walter Wainwright was just about to close his pharmacy. He stayed open late on Friday nights to oblige the rural population around the little town of Chowchilla. Business had been slow this night, but he had worked on the accounts and made out some orders. It was a little past his usual time for closing when he moved down the store to lock the front door. This warm August evening, the door had been propped open, and he was in the act of closing it when two men came pushing in, staggering him back.

"Here—what d'you want? I'm just closing—"

"You're closed, Pop!" One of them banged the door. In his confusion, Wainwright got only a vague impression of the pair—not men, kids—late teenagers, or the one perhaps a little older—nondescript jeans, T-shirts—one more blond and bigger than the other. They looked tough, menacing. "This is a heist, Pop. What've you got in the register?" The smaller one went back there, and Wainwright heard the cash register opened.

"Here, you can't—you get out—" The bigger one hit him and he was knocked down hard against the front counter. His glasses fell off. The big one began kicking him, as if on random impulse. It had all happened so suddenly that he couldn't think—he'd never been held up before, but he knew there were things he should remember—good look at them so he could give the sheriff a description—tell what had been taken—but they hadn't even showed a gun, and this couldn't happen to an ordinary respectable citizen in his own place— He was kicked savagely again, and he rolled over with a little moan.

"Hey, there's only about forty bucks here—"

"There might be some stuff in the back, reds or meth or something—"

Wainwright tried to get up. They were leaving—stamping loudly up the aisle past him—careless, thinking they'd put him out of action. But he wasn't—these louts of kids, think they could do anything they pleased—try to tell the sheriff what they looked like, anyway— With a superhuman effort he made it to his feet, staggered to the front door. In the quiet, deserted street outside he saw a car in front of Sam's English Tailor Shop next door. Its engine roared to life and it took off with a squeal of tires on asphalt. An old car—people in the front, in the back—

"About forty dollars," he told the sheriff feebly from his hospital bed later; he had a couple of broken ribs and assorted bruises. "And I'll have to check my records but I think they took some drugs—barbiturates and—"

"These Goddamn punk kids!" said the sheriff disgustedly.

They were free spirits like all the rock told it, they spent life as it moved them, thinking about tomorrow was a drag, take it as it happened.

Only sometimes Ollie thought about yesterdays. Some time awhile back—it had been February or May or some time, hot weather but that didn't mark a date in California—anyway, just after he'd taken up with Thor.

Thor Sigurdson. Maybe it wasn't a real name. But Thor was smart, he could figure things out. How to get the bread. Only just this last time those two other guys had kind of outsmarted them. All that loot—

Ollie did what Thor told him to because, well, Thor was that kind: you did what he said. But he didn't like to remember that time, awhile back, the boy set all afire with gasoline over his clothes. They'd only got about two dollars from him, and it was probably the stuff, whatever, barbs or meth, had set Thor kind of wild, to do a thing like that. Ollie didn't like to think about it. Mostly he didn't.

It had been before they picked up these two chicks. Su-Su and Tally. The chicks were all right. Tally was kind of weird, with those fortune-telling cards and all, but O.K.

Su-Su was a real fun girl, Thor said. She was Thor's girl, but that was O.K. with Ollie, he wouldn't come right out and say but he didn't care all that much about the sex stuff, and he guessed Tally didn't either.

Everybody said, freedom and do your own thing, but whatever, you had to have the bread, and right now they didn't. They'd only got about forty bucks from that guy, and time they got the tank filled back there and bought hamburgers, that was twelve-thirteen bucks of it gone.

The car was kind of beat-up but it went. It was Thor's car.

"Listen," said Thor. He was driving. "We could pull the same caper down in L.A. or some place. A bank guy—it's the way you do it now. Only we don't stay in the house, we take him some place."

"What place?" asked Su-Su. "We don't have a place in L.A."

"We'll get a place. I know a place—I been in L.A. before. A place we can go, all free spirits, nobody to ask any questions, see. It's a thing to do. Get a load of bread, friends. A real load." Thor was driving fast. Ollie thought Thor was a real handsome guy, and he guessed Su-Su thought so too. Thor was big and blond and strong and his beard was curly. Ollie couldn't grow a beard; he'd tried. Thor always had ideas.

"I'll lay out the cards on it," said Tally. She was sitting cross-legged in the back seat, shuffling those funny cards. "Only what'd I use for a Sig-Significator? The book says—"

Thor said what she could do with her cards. "They always *know*," said Tally.

The old car gave a lurch and Thor cussed, hit the brake. Su-Su let out a screech. But there wasn't anything around to hit, and Thor got the heap stopped finally. He and Ollie got out. It was the right front tire, blown all to hell.

"Christ damn the luck!" said Thor. The car was canted along the shoulder, but there wasn't any new damage. "The damn spare isn't much better. Ollie, get the jack."

"Sure, Thor."

It was a lonely stretch of road, a winding blacktop two-lane road in the middle of nowhere. The girls got out and watched while Ollie got the tire off and put on the spare. Su-Su's long blond hair blew wildly in the wind; after a while Tally got back in the car. "My God," said Su-Su, "it looks like the end of the world. Nobody—nothing—nowhere."

But there was a sign a little bit ahead, a regular highway sign. *Sauquit Point—Rte. 101, 1 mile.*

"We got to get some bread," said Thor. "It'll be easy— easy and cool, man. I still got the gun."

"Sure, man," said Ollie. "We'll do it."

They got back in the front seat. Tally was laying out her cards on top of her suitcase in back. "Wait a minute till I look, Thor—Oooh, the end card's the Five of Wands and I just don't like it, Thor—"

They were on their way again. Somewhere.

The twins were being put to bed.

"An' God bless Mama and Papa," thus Terry, piously.

"An' Bast an' Sheba an' Nefertite an' El Señor an' Cedric," chimed in Johnny. Mrs. MacTaggart regarded them approvingly. Their parents might be heathens, but at least she had seen that the twins were properly baptized into the fold; and if those same parents remained unaware of it, what the eye didn't see—

"An' Mairí, an' Cedric, an' Sheba—"

"I *said* Sheba an' Cedric!"

"Well, I didn't—"

"And what Luis would say!" exclaimed Alison. Mrs. MacTaggart was prudently silent. She had made at least one novena to coax her gallant Spanish man back into a state of grace; but he was a very obstinate sinner.

Two

On Saturday morning Mendoza came in at the usual time. He was slightly intrigued by the offbeat female on the freeway, and Grace had the witnesses coming in this morning. It was Sergeant Lake's day off, and Sergeant Farrell was sitting at the switchboard.

But the first witness who showed up was one of the owners of the liquor store heisted last Wednesday night; Higgins took him down to R. and I. to look at the mug shots. Hackett, coming in late and hearing about the girl on the freeway for the first time, was slightly intrigued too. "But we probably won't get an autopsy report till Monday now. It doesn't sound as if there'd be much to go on even if we identify her, if she was a drifter."

"See what the witnesses say," said Mendoza. "I know there's no sidewalk along the freeway, but the guardrail isn't all that close to the right lane. How'd she come to go over?"

"Oh," said Hackett after a moment. "Yes, I see. Did Jase—"

26-

"You want me?" Grace came in and shut the door behind him. "There's a citizen out there demanding to see the boss. Rory's trying to ease him out. Arnold Berry."

"Oh, hell," said Hackett. "We might have expected it, I saw three lines about that hearing on page eleven of the *Times* yesterday. But what he wants here— Facts of life, Luis, we can't waste time on it."

Mendoza sat up, looking annoyed. "Theoretically, Arturo, we are public servants. No, I don't want to see him—and as I recall he's not a very brainy citizen—but I'd better talk to him."

Hackett shrugged. "More fool you, better let Rory shoo him out. And I'm not sitting in on it."

"Maybe I can help you get rid of him after you've said all the words of one syllable," said Grace sadly, and stayed, hovering by the window. Mendoza put out his cigarette, looked at the pack of cards he'd just taken from the top drawer, put them back, lit another cigarette and stood up as the door opened. "Mr. Berry."

Arnold Berry was a nondescript balding man in his forties. Looking at him, Mendoza recalled this and that about him, feeling depressed. Berry was a clerk in a department store, men's furnishings, a respectable citizen, an anonymous man in the street, a little man; nobody except his immediate acquaintances would ever have known his name in the ordinary way. He'd been married to a nondescript quiet wife and had two children, girls ten and twelve, evidently as nondescript as their parents. He had a habit of going out to bowl once a week, which was the only reason he was in Mendoza's office now, alive. He sat down on invitation and looked at Mendoza angrily, accusingly.

"You *arrested* him," he said. "You told me it'd be a charge of murder. It *was* murder. Coldblooded murder."

"Mr. Berry, I told you we'd recommend that charge to

the District Attorney's office. Once we've made an arrest, the legal procedure is out of our hands. I saw the result of the hearing on Thursday, and I can only say—"

"We pay police to *punish* criminals," said Berry. "My God, I don't understand it—the doubletalk from that lawyer—it was *murder!*"

Grace shrugged at Mendoza. You could bandy the legal definitions around. But to all intents and purposes Joe Riley, who had deliberately and scientifically set fire to the apartment building where the Berrys—and three other families—had lived, had committed murder. Mrs. Berry, the two children, and another female tenant had all died in the fire.

"Mr. Berry, it's not up to the police to prosecute any charges. I sympathize with you, I know how you feel—"

"I don't see how they can do that. I tried to talk to the—the prosecuting lawyer, he said something about a bargain, I don't understand it—"

"Plea bargaining," said Grace gently. "To expedite cases before the court. There's always a backlog." But in practice, of course, it so often resulted in an automatic reduced charge.

"Murder," said Berry angrily. "And that judge just sent him up to Camarillo to be *examined*. By the head doctors. The other lawyer, he was mad—he said he could be out and loose on the streets in a month, on probation. These head doctors, they'll say nobody ever loved him or something and let him out—I know the damn guff they talk—"

And that was all too possible. "I realize how you must feel," repeated Mendoza formally, "but it's out of our hands once an arrest is made. The District—"

"You know how I *feel?*" said Berry loudly. "How the hell could you know how I feel? Police are supposed to protect honest people—not the criminals! What do you mean, you know how I feel? Damn you, nobody knows how I feel—my whole family *murdered* by that bastard, and nothing's going to happen to him at all, and you tell me the police can't do anything! I just wish—I just hope to God, if *you've* got any family—I'd like to see *you* lose them all, and see what you'd say then—"

"Now, Mr. Berry," began Grace, but Berry put his hands to his face and almost ran out to the corridor. Grace went after him. Their useful policewoman-secretary, neat blond Wanda Larsen, had just come in; seeing the distraught Berry she started for him, but he rushed past her and vanished down the hall. "What's all that?" asked Wanda, and sobered when Grace told her. "Poor man. You can imagine how he feels."

"I wonder," said Grace. "Can we? Exercise in empathy, lady."

There was still the eternal legwork to do on the heists, looking for men on record and hauling them in to question; Hackett and Higgins were out on that, and Palliser had gone out somewhere too. But Matt Piggott hung around to hear the witnesses on the new one; he and Grace would probably team up on that.

The witnesses were all female, from young to middle-aged, and reasonably intelligent; they told a story which agreed on all main points. All but one of them thought the driver had pushed the girl out of the car; it looked, at least, as if he'd been struggling with her. Definitely the driver was male; they hadn't got a good look, but were sure of that. No, he hadn't got out of the car. "I don't know why we didn't have a pile-up," said the car-pool driver with a shudder. "Just fool luck there wasn't a car behind me right then. He jammed on the brake, and so did I, I thought sure I was going to ram him, but I managed to stop about an inch from his rear bumper, and that's when he took off again. And with everything else to look at, you're asking what kind of car it was—well, I ask you!"

Grace and Piggott left them waiting for Wanda to

type the statements. "A funny thing all right," said Piggott. "Suppose they were both high on something? The type you said she looked like—" Back in Mendoza's office they found him eyeing a shabby canvas backpack on his desk.

"You said you'd brought it in. I take it, nothing for the lab." Mendoza prodded it fastidiously.

"I went through it looking for I.D. There's nothing there. Anonymous."

"Remnants of a life," said Mendoza, and opened it. The canvas was dirty and worn, one strap broken and mended with a couple of large safety pins. He upended the thing and its meager contents slid out onto the desk. An old Instamatic pocket camera, empty of film, a soiled white cotton dress, wrinkled, cheap quality when new; a pair of ancient jeans, two new-looking white T-shirts, a pair of sneakers, two pairs of white cotton ankle socks, a dime-store cosmetic bag containing three lipsticks, a soiled powder puff, and a small box of loose powder; a cheap gold necklace, broken; a rope of fake agate love beads; a pack of cigarettes nearly full.

"Pall Malls," said Mendoza. "*¿Pues qué?*" He inserted a long forefinger into the pack and slid a cigarette out. "But you can't always go by the label." He passed the cigarette to Grace: a loosely packed, ill-made cigarette, the paper yellowish and brittle.

"Oh, yes," said Piggott sadly. "The grass. Looking so innocent and ordinary." He shook his sandy head. "Right back to Sodom and Gomorrah."

The phone shrilled on the desk and Mendoza picked it up. "I've got Wilcox Street asking for you," said Farrell.

"Mendoza? Barth here. Say, it's possible we've got somebody here who can identify a body for you. The one you picked up in MacArthur Park. You sent up a description, and by what she says—"

"That'd be a step farther on."

"Yeah. A Mrs. Norcott, Amelia Norcott. Anyway, it sounded close enough that I've had Bob Laird take her down to the morgue. If she can identify, he'll fetch her in to your office."

"Thanks so much," said Mendoza absently.

Even as Palliser had figured, when he got to that Ford agency, they couldn't help him at all. Or rather, help Merced. The original agency owner, Bob Hauger, had retired last year and his son ran the place now, a big, florid, talkative man who was regretful that he couldn't help the police.

"But, my God, Sergeant, you can see for yourself, every car we get in here we put our plate frame on." He gestured. "It's good advertising, and doesn't cost all so much. Like, if you could tell me the make and model and year, I could give you some idea, if we sold it off the used lot or what, and when. But when all you've got is a car wearing our plate frame—"

"Yes, I see," said Palliser. He didn't know why Merced had bothered to pass the information on. Except, of course, he thought suddenly, that if the car had come from L.A. it might be heading back here—with that bunch of wild ones in it who had (Merced seemed to be convinced) left a messy multiple murder behind them. L.A. had enough wild ones here already, and it would be nice to pick up these particular ones. But if Merced couldn't offer any better leads, that didn't look likely.

He went back to the office and sent a telex up to Merced.

"I guess it was just fate or something," said Mrs. Amelia Norcott. "You can't say we didn't try." She sighed. She was a large-boned, rather handsome woman about fifty, and her plain tan dress and modest jewelry were in excellent taste. "What did he say your name is? Oh, yes. Well, Lieutenant Mendoza, it's just terrible to think of that happening to Linda, but I'll have to say I'm not surprised."

"Mrs. Norcott's identified the body as her niece, Linda Norcott," said Detective Laird of Wilcox Street. "It'll be in this, um, jurisdiction, you see, ma'am, so you just tell the lieutenant whatever you can."

"My husband's niece," said Mrs. Norcott. "And in the ordinary way, John would never have dreamed of asking me to come to such a place—that awful morgue, I mean— but he's in the hospital. He had a heart attack last month, he's doing fine, so they say, but he's still in the hospital. And when I was there last night, he showed me the piece in the paper about this girl's body being found, and it surely did sound like Linda. That is, any girl could be about five-five and slim and blond and in the early twenties and all, but it said there was this scar on her shoulder, and Linda— And John said it might be and we'd better find out. Just terrible, but maybe fate."

"You hadn't missed her, she hadn't been living with you?"

"Not for four years or so, since she was seventeen. You can't say we didn't try, and she was a good sweet youngster when we first had her—that's where she got that scar, in the accident when her mother and father were killed—John's brother Bill and his wife. Linda was only ten. We were glad to take her—none of our own, you know— and she was a nice child. It was when she got into high school she got in with a bad crowd—what young people are coming to nowadays—we couldn't believe it at first but she got on this awful dope, she got picked up by the police, running around with this wild crowd—and then she got pregnant. It was a terrible worry—we were ashamed,

32-

John felt just awful about it—but I can't feel, and he had to say too, it was any of our fault. She got in with a bad crowd—"

"We'll probably have something on her," Laird interjected. "She was living with the Norcotts then—Hillside Avenue." That was a solidly good middle-class address in Hollywood, but as both he and Mendoza knew, backgrounds said nothing these days.

"The baby was put up for adoption. We didn't know where Linda was half the time, and then she went off and we never saw her for months. No, I don't know where she'd been living lately—she came asking for money sometimes, and John couldn't help but remember she was his own family, he'd usually give her some. The last time we saw her, let's see, it was late in June. She came to the house—"

"Alone? In a car?"

"There was a man in the car, he didn't come in. I don't think she had a car, it was probably his. I didn't get a look at him." She didn't know any names to tell them, any of Linda's recent friends; after listening to a little more of the same, Mendoza thanked her and said Laird would drive her back to Hollywood. "Well, John said we'd better find out. A terrible thing, but maybe a blessing in disguise. Poor girl, I'm sure she couldn't have been very happy."

Farrell checked with Wilcox Street for any record, and they sent the package down to greet Mendoza when he came back from lunch. Nobody else from the office had been at Federico's; presumably they were all out chasing down heist-men. But Palliser came in just after Mendoza, and heard about Linda.

"Expectable record," said Mendoza, glancing over it. "Narco, D. and D. twice, narco, one count of soliciting.

More to the point, names of some known associates. She was picked up the latest time a couple of weeks ago for possession."

"Out on bond, of course," said Palliser.

"*¿Cómo no?* Naturally. We can have a look for these boyfriends. Ron Talliaferro, Jack Dosser, Randy Greenwald—last known addresses appended, they've all got little rap-sheets too. Dosser was picked up with her once."

"Thanks so much," said Palliser. "The little worthless punks—and she wasn't much loss either."

"But somebody did strangle her and we're supposed to find out who, if possible. Where is everybody?"

"Chasing down heisters, I suppose. Unless something new went down." Palliser took the list of addresses and went out, passing Higgins on the way in.

"Like to help me lean on one, Luis?" Higgins looked tired; it had turned hotter today.

The hunt for the heist-men was complicated, of course, by the fact that all the jobs hadn't been pulled by the same ones. It looked fairly certain that it had been the same pair who had held up victims on the street on two occasions; but it could have been ten different men who had pulled the other jobs—four liquor stores, a pharmacy, a small market, and two dairy stores. On four of those jobs witnesses said there had been two men; the others had been loners. The descriptions were vague; descriptions so often were. The only useful one they had came from three witnesses to one of the dairy store jobs, who said the heist-man was a little fellow, short and slender. It was definite that at least four of them were Negro. But there were a lot of men turned up by the computer down in R. and I. who had records of heists, and it was a long job hunting them.

The latest one Higgins had picked up was typical: Emilio Gonzales, record back to age fourteen, just off P.A.

for burglary. He'd been questioned before, by a lot of cops, and he knew they hadn't anything on him. He went on saying sullenly, "I don't know nothin' about what you're talkin' about. I ain't done nothin'." Finally they let him go; and he could be one of those they wanted, but there was nothing to say yes or no. The thankless job could also be very tiresome.

Without much expectation, Mendoza called Dr. Bainbridge's office and got one of his bright young surgeons. "Oh, the accident victim? Young girl—well, I took it as an accident, the way the body's smashed up. Or suicide."

"That's what we'd like to know, Doctor. You haven't done the autopsy yet?"

"No, of course not. First come, first served, Lieutenant. There was a woman identified that other body, I suppose you know. I was about to get to that. We'll probably have a report for you by Monday."

"So, paciencia," said Mendoza to himself, and went home early. He found his household unexpectedly quiet; Mrs. MacTaggart had taken the twins to a children's cartoon matinee. Alison was busy over a letter in what was supposed to be Mendoza's den. "Letter from the Lockharts," she reported, smiling. "They've got a new granddaughter."

Mendoza only grunted. And if it hadn't been for that shrewd ex-cop John Lockhart, he wouldn't have his household full of hostages to fortune. He read the letter absently and handed it back, stripping off his tie. He realized suddenly that Arnold Berry had been at the back of his mind all day, and told Alison about that.

"¿Qué puede uno hacer?" said Alison soberly. "Poor man—poor people. What could you say to him? But it does make you wild to think of one like that—Luis."

"¿Cómo?"

"I know you think it's silly, but it makes me feel—a

little scared," said Alison. "We've got much. Too much. Sometimes I feel as if Fate is just waiting to—to—"

"As Johnny would say, *estúpido*." Mendoza grinned at her, his redhaired Scots-Irish girl.

"No, but I do. When you think how lucky we've been—"

"Don't borrow trouble, *hermosa*. Has that mocking bird turned up yet?" Their little feathered friend, usually active at this season dive-bombing the cats, was unaccountably absent.

"No, and I really think something must have happened to him. Maybe he died of old age," said Alison hopefully. "I'd hate to think a cat got him."

"Not one of ours, anyway. The only successful hunter is Bast, and she always brings her catch home, to show off."

The night watch came on—Conway, Schenke, Galeano. Conway had been temporarily shifted from day watch while Shogart was on vacation, and was feeling disgruntled about it. "Just about get used to sleeping all morning when E. M.'ll get back," he said, yawning. "Take any bets we get another heist tonight?"

"No bets," said Galeano. He was back to smoking again, and with difficulty had shed the ten extra pounds. "And to think of Tom off with that cute blonde, out of the heat wave somewhere— When are you going to marry your lady cop, Rich?"

"No way," said Conway darkly. He'd been dating one of the girls at Wilcox Street, Margot Swain. "I'm backing off from that one, she's a little too eager. I'm not ready to settle down yet, and look who's talking." Galeano and Schenke were both bachelors too.

"I'll tell you, though," said Schenke thoughtfully, "I've got a kind of idea that Henry's nosing around our Wanda. I know he's taken her out."

"She's a nice girl," said Conway indifferently; and the phone rang on Galeano's desk.

"Here we go. Robbery-Homicide, Galeano . . . Yeah . . . Got it. Broadway and Ninth? We'll be on it. You called it, Rich. Another heist." He got up. The phone rang on Conway's desk and he picked it up, waving Galeano out.

"Robbery-Homicide, Conway."

"I've got Sacramento on the line," said the desk sergeant downstairs. "A Sergeant Aiken."

Conway wondered what this was about. In a moment a heavy bass voice introduced itself as Aiken, and Conway asked, "What can L.A. do for you, Sergeant?"

"A little legwork," said Aiken. "You know this bank caper we had last week—manager's wife held hostage, and fifty G's in loot. Well, the Feds got it back, but it was a fairly stupid job. We picked up a good set of latents off the coffee table in the living room—they held her in her own house—and NCIC made them. Roderick Pratt, little record around Frisco for B. and E., armed robbery—he's just out from a one-to-three in Vacaville. We put out the word, and a pigeon fingered him about two hours ago. We've pulled him in."

"Congratulations."

"Yeah, but there were three of 'em, so Mrs. Thirkell says—the bank manager's wife. We've been prodding at Pratt, and he just decided to tell us something. He didn't have the bright idea, so he says. It was a pal of his he met in the joint, Joel Fliegel. And he says Fliegel's headed down your way, maybe there now. He's got a wife in L.A. and he wants to get her to come back to him."

"Oh, yes? How'd you get the loot back?"

"They aren't very bright, as I say," said Aiken with a laugh. "They told Thirkell to leave the bag with the money in a public phone-booth in a shopping center. The Feds were keeping an eye on it, naturally, and so were we, and

-37

when this character walked off with it the Feds were on him and he spotted them. Dropped it and ran. We don't know who he was—it was the third man. Pratt claims he doesn't know either, said he was a guy Fliegel knew, and he only knows him as Siggy. The only description we've got, he's got a beard."

"Which is fairly common these days," said Conway. "Have you got an address for Fliegel's missus?"

"Yeah, Vacaville had it in their records. She's a Verna Fliegel, address on Hoover Street."

Conway took that down. "So we'll see if Fliegel has arrived."

"We'd be obliged if you can pick him up. Pratt says he took the heap they were using. It's a 1957 Dodge four-door, white over blue, registered to Fliegel. The plate's DGM-790, the old one, orange on black."

"Thank you so much. We'll have a look," said Conway. Schenke and Galeano had both gone out on the heist. It was probable that Mrs. Verna Fliegel had a job somewhere, and unless she was a cocktail waitress or a go-go dancer might be at home now. He went down to the lot for his car and drove up to the address on Hoover. It was a shabby old two-story apartment house. Verna Fliegel was listed in apartment twelve, but he got no answer to the bell. There was a row of garages behind the building, but only one was open and that contained an old Buick convertible. There was a resident manageress on the ground floor but she wasn't at home either.

Frustrated, Conway went back to the office and left a note for the day watch.

Hackett had told Higgins about Arnold Berry's visit, and when Higgins came out to get his car on Sunday morning he found he was thinking about that, suddenly. What could you say to Berry? Higgins thought superstitiously that maybe he'd been too lucky, that Fate was just waiting to show him who was boss. Anything could happen to anybody.

His family was all accounted for, this hot still morning—the family he'd been so long without. Bert Dwyer's good kids—Bert had been a friend of his, and he liked to think maybe Bert was glad he was taking care of the kids. And Mary. His pretty gray-eyed Mary was out in the back yard, weeding a bed of geraniums, and his firsthand family, plump Margaret Emily, was tottering unsteadily around the patio; she's just started to walk. Steve was already shut up in the darkroom Higgins had contrived in the garage, and Laura was loud at piano practice in the house. The little black Scottie Brucie bounced around Mary.

Higgins suddenly walked back from the garage to kiss her again. "Well, what prompted that?" asked Mary, smiling.

"Just wild impulse."

When he got to the office he found Mendoza and Hackett talking about the overnight call from Sacramento. "I checked our records, we haven't anything on her," said Hackett. "I suppose we might find her home on Sunday. She could be willing to cooperate and tip us off if Fliegel shows up."

"Could be," agreed Higgins. "Quiet night?"

"Another heist." Mendoza looked annoyed, lighting another cigarette, swiveling around in his desk chair. "Couple on the way home from a movie, held up in the street. No description—it was dark—except, he was big and probably Negro. He got twelve bucks and some change."

"Gun or knife?" asked Higgins.

"A knife."

"Well, that makes a little change." All of the heisters

they were looking for had had guns, except one. "Think it could tie up to the other one?" That had been a week ago, a gas-company employee held up at knife-point at a parking lot on Hill.

Hackett groaned. "Up in the air. Could be, couldn't be. It—"

"—was dark," said Higgins. "Well, I'll see if I can locate this Fliegel female. Be a little change from the heisters."

"There is also Linda," said Mendoza. "As John said, small loss, but we are paid to hunt the fellows in black hats. We want to talk to these recent boyfriends—one of them may have strangled her in a fit of temper, for some reason. Or no reason. And Art gives us the word for ninety percent of what we see—the stupidity and/or cupidity."

That was the word for it. Higgins went out again, into ninety-eight-degree heat, to the address on Hoover. He didn't find Verna Fliegel. The manageress was now home, and she told him that Mrs. Fliegel worked at Robinson's downtown, and that was all she knew about her. She was a quiet tenant, always paid the rent promptly. Yes, she had a car, but the manageress couldn't say what it was, a little car.

She ought to be home sometime today, or they could catch her at her job tomorrow.

They never saw Piggott on Sunday until after church. When Higgins looked in, Mendoza was sitting at his desk, cigarette in mouth corner, shuffling the deck of cards. He listened to what Higgins had to say and said, "So you might have a look round for Linda's boyfriends, George. John's out looking for that Greenwald. And I am still feeling slightly curious about our latest Jane Doe, with the pseudo Pall Malls. Not very, just some."

"It's building up to a new heat wave," said Higgins. "Did you say we had addresses for the boyfriends?"

"Jimmy's got them." Mendoza started to deal poker hands. "Just possibles, but we'd better talk to them."

Resignedly Higgins applied to Lake and was given the addresses from Wilcox Street's records of one Jack Dosser, little record of possession, purse-snatching, one B. and E. The address was on Cornwell in Boyle Heights. He drove over there; it was an old single house, in falling-down condition, ramshackle, one front window broken, unpainted for years. The wooden porch gave ominously under Higgins' bulk; he pushed the bell and waited five minutes before he finally roused a thin slatternly-looking woman who looked at the badge in his hand unemotion-ally.

"So what's he done now?" she asked.

"We just want to talk to him," said Higgins. "Jack Dosser. He's your son? Is he here?"

"He's here. He's usual here, is he broke. Which he mostly is. I figure it's like a con-game, cop."

"What?" said Higgins.

"Life. If some God made it up, He's a con artist. Ro-mance an' true love! You meet up with it, he's a drunk an' a bum, an' he leaves you with a dopey bum for a kid. So what the hell? I was a damn fool an' worked for a living till last year—get as much on the welfare now. An' he isn't gonna get no more of it. You want him, you take him, cop."

Higgins found Jack Dosser asleep in a dirty back bed-room, and took him back to the office. Dosser didn't seem to be high on anything at the moment, or even burdened with a hangover. He was rational, and alarmed and sur-prised at being hauled in. He was a big paunchy fellow in his twenties, with a feeble attempt at a beard and a slack mouth.

Palliser had just come back to the office. He had fin-ally located Greenwald in the Alameda jail, where he'd been since last Monday night, booked on a charge of burglary.

They settled Dosser in an interrogation room and asked him when he'd seen Linda Norcott last.

"Linda?" said Dosser. He looked even more surprised. "I don't know anything about Linda. I haven't seen her in a while—what's with Linda?" But he was scared; he looked at the two big cops and licked his lips and fidgeted. Higgins and Palliser felt encouraged; maybe they had something here. Maybe they were about to close out this Murder One, what it looked like.

"Last Tuesday night, Dosser," said Higgins. "Were you—"

"Tuesday?" said Dosser. "It was Thursday—I—how'd you *know?* How'd you know it was me? I didn't really mean to—to hurt nobody, I just needed some bread—I useta know a girl worked for the phone company, and they keep real crazy shifts—I know there's a shift off at eleven, an' I waited in that parking lot— How'd you know it was me heisted them two girls?"

Higgins and Palliser looked at each other. "And if Matt was here," said Palliser, "he'd remind us that the guilty flee where no man pursueth. Of all the silly coincidences—" But it was nice to have something cleared up.

---------------------------- Three

Fiction tended to glamorize the job. Too often it was just slogging routine, which was anathema to Mendoza; but the long years of discipline were behind him. He went out on the hunt for the men from records, and at getting on for three that afternoon came up with what might be a jackpot. Yesterday afternoon the liquor store owner had tentatively picked out the mug shot of one Buck Rainey as one of the pair who had held up the store last Wednesday night; Hackett had drawn blank on him once, but Mendoza found him at the address they had for one of his ex-girl-friends, and brought him in.

Rainey was black, belligerent, and a good deal bigger than Mendoza, and there wasn't anybody else in to help lean on him. Mendoza stashed him in an interrogation room and asked Lake where everybody was.

"How should I know? Jase and John went out on a new call—yeah, a corpse. Somewhere down on Alpine. I haven't laid eyes on Art or George since before lunch."

Balefully Sergeant Lake eyed the remains of his lunch in the wastepaper-basket, an empty carton that had held cottage cheese. The sedentary years had been catching up to him lately. "Leave him to cool a while, somebody may come back to help scare him." A minute later the switchboard buzzed at him and he plugged in. "Well, there's an excuse to take a breather. Chief of police in Merced on the line."

Mendoza went into the office and picked up the phone. "Lieutenant Mendoza, Robbery-Homicide."

The voice on the phone was mild and rather slow: it built a picture in Mendoza's mind of an elderly man, deceptively quiet, probably shrewd. "Pomeroy," it said. "Chief of police up here, Lieutenant. I hope you've been seeing the reports on our Murder One. It's been kind of a thing."

"It sounds that way."

"Never had anything like it here in my time, and I've been on this force going on twenty-eight years. Hell of a thing—whole family killed, a damn bloody business, and what we've sorted out, no rhyme or reason to it. Our doctor—Dr. Hopeson, he hasn't got a head doctor's degree maybe but his head's screwed on pretty tight, and he thinks this bunch were high on dope of some kind—the acid maybe. It was a mess, Lieutenant. And Jim Goodman and his wife nice people, the girls not wild or anything."

"That license-plate frame was N.G.," said Mendoza.

"Yeah, we got your telex. I just thought it was a chance, but I can see, big place like that, there'd be no lead. And if the car came from L.A., that doesn't say it's headed back down there."

"God forbid," said Mendoza.

"Yeah. Well, if I can ask you to cooperate, Lieutenant, I've got a couple of witnesses I'd like to bring down there for a session with your artists."

"Oh?" Mendoza regarded the phone with mild interest, lighting a cigarette one-handed. "You're closer to Frisco, Chief."

"I know it," said Pomeroy dryly, "and every once in a while we have to use their forensic lab or something. I guess those boys are O.K., but I happen to know your boys are something else. Kind of pioneers in a lot of different aspects of the job, hah? If you don't mind, I'd like to see what your artists might come up with. We did what we could with the Identikit but the witnesses say it isn't much good."

"Well, we can try to oblige you. Somebody gave you descriptions—good enough for a composite drawing, you think?"

"Could be. The next-door neighbors. See, the two older girls had evidently picked up these characters at The Peach Tree—roadhouse where a lot of the kids hang out, quiet place as a rule, no trouble. Anybody's guess what happened in that house, but the neighbors—Don and Wilma Finley—saw that bunch go in, with the Goodman girls. It was a nice warm night, about nine o'clock, they were on the front porch—yard lights on, theirs and the Goodmans'. They thought it was a funny-looking crowd for the girls to be bringing home—city-looking beatnik kids, the beard and all. They can't give us any names, but they had a pretty good look at the two men, if not the girls with 'em. Little bit past teenage maybe, one of the men bigger than the other, and a beard. I'd just like to see what an artist might come up with. I'd like to catch up with these—unholy bastards. There wasn't even a fight, looks like they come back after the family was asleep and just went berserk. Occurs to me, Lieutenant, taking that license-plate frame, if we get any kind of picture we might look at some of the mug shots you got down there. Could be we'd hit a jackpot."

"Well, you're welcome to come and try," said Mendoza.

"Figure the city can run to a motel bill," said Pomeroy. "Probably be down some time tomorrow, thanks, Lieutenant."

Mendoza went out to see if any of his wandering boys had come back, and found Matt Piggott chatting with Lake. "I've been wasting the day," he complained. "One of the things about these punks—they don't stay anywhere. You pin down an address for them and next time you want to talk to them they're long gone to some other cheap pad."

Mendoza laughed. "Just one of the problems. So you can come and help scare Rainey."

That was a little exercise in futility too. Rainey said he was clean, hadn't done nothing, never was nowhere near that liquor store Wednesday night. But he couldn't or wouldn't say where he'd been instead; of course last Wednesday night was awhile ago to one like Rainey, and maybe he honestly didn't remember. Anyway, he didn't have an alibi, and the owner had picked out his mug shot, so they'd keep him, and arrange a lineup for tomorrow, see if the store owner could pick him out. He protested volubly, but Piggott took him over to the Alameda jail.

"Did I tell you about the new one?" asked Lake.

"You'd just started to."

"It was something to do with the Fire Department. John was just in, he went out on it with Jase."

"The Fire Department?" said Mendoza. "*¿Qué sé yo?*"

Palliser had found Ron Talliaferro, said to be an erstwhile boyfriend of Linda Norcott's, after a time-consuming hunt. Talliaferro had been sharing a small apartment with a pal in Hollywood, but the pal, luckily at home, said he'd moved out a couple of months back, and probably had moved in with Jeanie. Jeanie Meyers, he couldn't give an address but he thought she worked at the drugstore on the corner of Vine and Santa Monica. Palliser asked around there and found her, a slightly overplump blonde who looked vague at the mention of the name and said, "Ron? Oh, *Ron.* Oh, gee, I haven't seen him in a while. What you want him for?"

"Just to talk to," said Palliser.

"Well, I dunno—you might ask Kurt. Kurt Rees. He works the same place Ron used to, he might know."

"Where's that?" There hadn't been any mention of a job in Talliaferro's rap-sheet, but he had held jobs off and on.

"Oh, it's a car-wash place out Vermont, the Quick and Easy."

There, Palliser finally found Talliaferro, as well as Rees; they were sharing an apartment. Talliaferro was much what Palliser had expected from the rap-sheet, a tall, immature-looking young fellow with fierce sideburns, a loose mouth, and a nervous laugh. He shied away from the badge and said hurriedly he was real clean.

"Just a few questions," said Palliser. "When did you see Linda Norcott last?"

"Linda? Oh, hell, quite awhile, I guess. I hadn't seen Linda in— Why? What's with Linda? She's a good enough chick but she flies a little too high for me, you know, man? Like I mean, you gotta have the bread, make it with Linda baby."

"Is that so. Did you see her last Tuesday night?"

"Tuesday? Hell, no, man. Tuesday—oh, sure, Tuesday, that's right, I was with Kurt and this pair of chicks, matter of fact mostly all night. Why? What am I s'posed to—"

Kurt Rees backed that up and added the names of the girls. The routine was usually tiresome, but it had to be done. Palliser walked back a block to where he'd left the Rambler and drove back downtown.

At least these days they weren't spending time writing reports. Their secretary was off on Sunday but Palliser left the gist of all that in a note on her desk, to be typed into a proper report tomorrow. He came out to the anteroom to find Jason Grace contemplating a manila folder just sent up from R. and I.

"If you ask me," said Grace in his soft voice, "I think there are too many people off on vacation at once in this place." He handed the folder to Palliser. It was a belated report: fingerprints of an unidentified body dispatched from the morgue now identified in their own records as those of Linda Norcott, record package enclosed.

"So we'd have got on it eventually," said Palliser, "but I can't say I'm much interested in how Linda came to get taken off, and it doesn't look as if our immediate leads are any use." He passed on the news about Talliaferro. "But that was the damnedest thing about her other boyfriend, that Dosser. Coming apart like that—the one held up those phone-company girls."

"I heard. Art talking about coincidence. Funny," agreed Grace, and Sergeant Lake looked up and announced that he had the Fire Department asking for somebody here.

"What for?" Palliser took the phone. "Robbery-Homicide, Sergeant Palliser."

"Division Captain Mummery, Station ninety-two, Sergeant. We're out on routine inspection, and we just came across a body. We thought you'd like to know."

"Where?"

Mummery gave him an address out past the railroad yards. "My God," he said, "wait till you see it. These people! We'd like to locate the owner to give him a citation, talk about fire hazard, but ten to one he's long gone. Place run down past fixing up, taxes still due, they just walk away. And the creeps take over."

"One of those." That was happening in the older parts of the city, and not much anybody could do about it. "O.K., we'll be on it."

The heat had probably gone over a hundred degrees today. They took the Rambler; Palliser refused to squeeze his six feet into Grace's little racing Elva. These old narrow streets the other side of the Southern Pacific yards were squalid, dirty, and the air seemed even more stagnant. On the block where the red fire truck was parked there were old frame houses on either side, mostly small bungalows, half of them empty and derelict; one was partly burned. But at the end of the street was a much larger two-story place. It was, they saw, the ghost of what had been, eighty-odd years ago, a fine town house of Victorian vintage. It had a cupola, and a wide porch on two sides, and there had been fussy gingerbread around the eaves, most of it broken away now. The few remnants of paint left had faded to no color, and most of the front windows were broken or cracked. Where there had once been a terraced lawn was bare dirt, with a fine crop of yellow mustard-weed at one side. On the porch stood or sat a motley little crowd of people, all young.

"My good God," said Grace. The man from the fire truck came to meet them. "Is it a commune?"

"Just a bunch of free spirits," said one of the firemen seriously. "Or they'd probably have got rid of the body before now. The drifters looking for free rent. You know the type—and the places like this."

"For our sins," said Grace. In this sordid dirty street his neat elegance looked out of place. "Where is it?"

"Upstairs—back room to the right. Could be an O.D., the autopsy will tell you."

The people on the porch moved aside silently to let

them pass. Glancing at them, Palliser was inclined to agree with the diagnosis: not one of the beat communes. Inhabitants of those places tended to conform rigidly in dress, and at first sight of a cop came out with the automatic names. These kids—well, up to their twenties—looked like the drifters all right, the new generation wandering around the country, footloose, doing their thing.

The body, on a thin mattress on the bare floor of the room upstairs, was that of a white male about twenty: rather an emaciated body, which was easy to see because it was stark naked. At first glance there wasn't anything else in the room.

"He hasn't been dead long," said Palliser. "Not twelve hours. If he had been it wouldn't have taken the Fire Department to find him. Looks like an O.D. all right." There wasn't a mark on the body; it was just dead.

There didn't seem to be much point in calling up the lab; it was a million to one there'd be any good latents to be lifted here. The room looked as if it hadn't been cleaned in years. They went downstairs and told the firemen to call an ambulance, and started to ask questions of the little crowd.

"Just get it *out* of here!" said the rather pretty dark girl Grace talked to first. "Nobody knew it was there, honest to Pete! Honestly! A body, for God's sake!" She was about twenty, with a nice tan and her hair in casual long braids; she had on a just-barely-there pink halter top and jeans. "No, I—we didn't know the guys in that room, who pays attention? People come and go. Me and Joy've been here, oh, I guess about a week—Joy Hall, that's her there in the bathing suit—we hitched up from Florida. I never been in L.A. before, but Joy knows people here. Somebody told us about this pad, a good deal, if there's a room empty you just move in. No trouble, nobody bothers you. One guy tried to get smart but I clobbered him."

It turned out that most of the ground-floor rooms were occupied. Not everybody was home. There wasn't a stove in the kitchen, and water and electricity were turned off. There were primitive cooking arrangements in a few rooms, camp stoves, charcoal grills: and most of them had a supply of candles. In one upper room they found two kerosene lamps and about ten gallons of kerosene in cans. "It's a wonder the damn place hasn't burned down," said Grace.

"Oh, we're as careful as can be." The young man who'd followed them upstairs again smiled at him winningly. "It's really not too bad at all." He was blond and graceful, and looked a little cleaner than anybody else here. "It's not at all bad, and offers absolute freedom, you see. And one can go uptown to one of those Turkish bath places every day. Willy and I've quite enjoyed being here. You don't have to mix with anybody else unless you want to." In a primitive way, the room offered comfort: a rickety old double bed, a few blankets, throw cushions on the floor, a tape recorder. "But I will say, it is inconvenient with no plumbing. There's a sanitary trench in back, but it's not really nice. We've been looking for a better place, where there'd be a few modern comforts, you know." He simpered at Palliser.

"Good God, what a hellhole," said Palliser, outside again. Nobody they talked to could tell them who the body might have been. Two fellows had been living in that room, not very long, and nobody had heard their names or exchanged any talk with them. But there were other guys staying here, not here now—might be back tonight or not—maybe they'd know. Most of those here now had been eager for a look at the corpse, and vaguely identified it as one of those fellows in that room.

"Natural in a way," said Grace. "Most of 'em wouldn't be here much. Place to sleep for no rent." The mysterious thing about the new generation was that most of them seemed to have money, or at least to get along without much trouble. There would be longsuffering parents who still supplied allowances; there was a lot of petty thievery and shoplifting. Some of them stayed in one place long enough to get on the welfare rolls.

The ambulance came and took the body away. "In a kind of way," said Grace, looking at the old house, "you can sympathize with whatever owner just walked away from here. Some other landlords are still trying to hang on, take the same types as these who'll pay something."

And this would make another report for Wanda to type. Unless somebody somewhere had the corpse's fingerprints on file, he might never get identified.

After wasting most of the day on the legwork, Higgins went back to Verna Fliegel's address about four o'clock and this time found her in. She looked at the badge with interest and asked him in; it was an old apartment but very tidy and clean, and she looked like the upright respectable citizen. She was about thirty-five, tall and thin, once very pretty; she was still good-looking, dark hair in a neat tailored cut, black harlequin glasses. Higgins, who harbored what Mary said were some oldfashioned notions, almost forgave her the mannishly cut navy pantsuit.

"I suppose it's about Joel," she said. "Sit down. Somebody passed the word to you boys that he's after me to go back to him. So I suppose you want him for something again."

"That's right," said Higgins. "Or rather not us. Sacramento."

She lit a cigarette before he could get out his lighter. "They grow cops as big as you up there? You don't say. Well, I'm not surprised. That cops want him again, I mean. With me, it was once bit twice shy, if you want to know. They do say, every dog allowed one bite. I didn't like it when he got picked up for burglary, the year after we were married, but I try to be a good Catholic and I was willing to give him another chance. But when he got in trouble again I'd had enough. By then I'd found out— that sergeant up there told me—he'd already had a record when I married him." She smiled wryly.

"Has he contacted you recently, Mrs. Fliegel?"

She nodded. "I didn't know any cops were after him or I'd have called you. He phoned me last Thursday, begged to come and see me. I told him no, we were finished like I told him last time. But he was here, waiting on the doorstep, when I got home on Friday. Well, of course I didn't like it—I was mad. I didn't want to let him in, but I didn't want an argument out in the hall either. I knew if I got past him and slammed the door on him, he'd go on ringing the bell and doing his sob-stuff, please come back darling, and all the neighbors— So I told him if he didn't go right away and leave me alone, I'd call the police."

"And that did it?"

"It sure did. I should have been smart enough to figure then that you were already after him. Well, I used to feel sorry for him, but what's the percentage?" She put out her cigarette with a sigh. "You'll never change that kind. What's he done now?"

"He was in on a bank robbery up in Sacramento—he and a couple of others took the manager's wife hostage."

"Getting into the big time, is he? I suppose you want me to let you know if he shows up again. I will, Sergeant, but I don't think it's very likely. I guess he knows I meant it."

"Does he have any friends around here? Anybody he

might go to for help? The word we have, they didn't get any of the loot, it was all recovered, and he might be broke."

"Well, I can't think of anybody. We came down here after he got out that first time, make a fresh start, you know? He did have a job here for a while—that was me, keeping his nose to the grindstone. He's a good mechanic, oddly enough. He worked for Buckley's garage down on Western. Come to think, I've got no idea whether they know there that he's got a record. He could have gone there."

"Well, thanks very much anyway," said Higgins, "and if you do hear from him you'll let us know." They had an A.P.B. out on Fliegel's car, having the plate-number from Sacramento.

By the time he got back to the office and sent the gist of that in a telex up to Sacramento, it was nearly the end of shift, too late to go out on anything else. He looked up the number of that garage and tried it, but the phone buzzed emptily at him: these days, businesses closed promptly on time.

Grace and Palliser were in, Piggott poring over a book at his desk; Hackett was on the phone. Higgins heard about the new body, and the aborted leads on Linda.

"One like that, who knows what happened," he said. "She had a record of soliciting. Could be she picked up a nut."

"Very possible," agreed Palliser.

"What's so interesting, Matt? Oh, your fish." Higgins peered over Piggott's shoulder at the colored illustration.

"Hum?" Piggott looked up. "Well, they're interesting. Such pretty little things. After all the not-so-pretty things we see all the time."

Hackett put the phone down and stood up. "That's that. Lineup set up for tomorrow morning, see if we can get a positive make on Rainey. Progress, possibly. I'm going home. What a life."

Hackett went home, to his Angel and Mark and his darling Sheila who was now running around on certain plump legs. Higgins went home to his belatedly acquired family. Palliser went home in time, as a cooperative and responsible husband, to finish bathing the baby David Andrew while Roberta got on with dinner. Piggott took the new book about tropical fish home to show Prudence; her mother was coming to dinner and she'd be interested too. Jason Grace went home to play with fat brown Celia Anne for half an hour before her bedtime, with Virginia busy in the kitchen.

And Mendoza went home to be coralled by his belated offspring before he could locate Alison to kiss her. "Come listen to me read, Daddy! Mama says I read good —*muy bueno!*" "I read better as Johnny, Daddy—*I* want to read to you—"

"One at a time, *niños!*" But they dragged him down to the nursery imperatively. The nursery was outgrowing the name, which the twins despised; and in fact a probable major crisis was looming, Alison talking about separating them into their own rooms. That would have to be done sometime, but they weren't going to like it.

"Listen to me, Daddy! Boys como first—I get to read first!"

The McGuffey primer and first reader had certainly been an inspiration, and by now, not quite officially four, the twins were reading with fair efficiency. But Johnny hadn't staggered through Lesson Twenty-seven about Fanny's doll when his sister wrenched the book from him forcibly.

"*¡Estúpido!* You say A 'stead of O! Listen to me, Daddy—"

Well, Alison could joke about the offspring of elderly parents being smarter, but there was no doubt that the twins were something special.

"'Here, take this little chick back under your wing! How safe the little chick feels now!' Don't I read good, Daddy?"

"*Muy bueno*, Terry."

He escaped when Mrs. MacTaggart came in to supervise their baths, and wandered out to the kitchen. Their shaggy dog Cedric offered him a polite paw. A steady crunching from the service porch signaled that at least one cat was augmenting dinner with Little Friskies. Alison was just taking a casserole out of the oven.

"Good day, *amado?*"

"A funny day. Other people's work. And frustrations—but it's a frustrating job." He opened the cupboard over the sink and took down the bottle of rye, and their alcoholic cat, El Señor of the Siamese-in-reverse mask, appeared out of nowhere to beg his share. Mendoza laughed and poured him an ounce in a saucer.

"Listen," said Ollie nervously, "listen, Thor, I guess you better do that part."

"Oh, for Gossakes! All you got to do—"

"Well, listen, man, but you said, like look for a name on a door, and I don't always read print so good. I guess you better go. Or one of the girls."

"Jeez, you can't do anything, can you. All right, all right." Thor was still mad. Ollie was sorry, but he figured he'd better say right out about the reading. If they were going to do it right. Thor was kind of mad at the girls too, because they'd had a fight about the money for this place. There were places they could have gone—Tally said that—like, for no rent. Places left empty, just move in. But Thor knew about this place, he'd been here before. Ten bucks it cost to move in, for a week and they wouldn't be here longer than that. He said, stupid Goddamn bitches, don't think ahead. Have to have a toilet, and a key to the door. If they were going to do it right. A lot of loot, if they did it right. Ollie hadn't thought about that either, but he kind of saw what Thor meant.

"You think you got enough sense to go get some hamburgers?" said Thor now, rough and still mad. He gave Ollie five bucks.

"Sure. Sure, man, I'll go do that. You want some french fries too? All the fixings."

"There's a place up the block on Sunset."

"Sure."

Su-Su was fooling with her hair in front of the mirror. "Hamburgers are fattening," she said. "I want a malt. A vanilla malt, Ollie. Thor dearest darling, you got maybe just one stick left?"

"No, and I got no bread for none till we pull this. You shut up."

Tally was laying out those silly cards. She didn't say anything. Ollie went out to get the hamburgers. He sure hoped this caper would go off nice and easy, like Thor said. Get all the bread. And it felt kind of exciting, doing the real bigtime thing. Thor was smart, he knew how to plan things.

When Conway came in, a little late, he had a postcard from Landers to hand around, from Santa Rosa. "Hope you're having fun playing cops and robbers," it said briefly in Landers' slanted backhand. "We're having fun too. Home on weekend probably and back to grind next week unless we decide to take off for Tahiti. Phil says tell Margot if at first you don't succeed—meaning—????"

-57

"That girl will get you yet, Rich," said Galeano.

"I'm a slippery customer," Conway said, grinning. "Take a bet?"

"No way. Did the day watch leave us anything?" For once they hadn't.

At ten-forty they had a call from a black-and-white on regular tour. Conway and Schenke went out on it, and were surprised and pleased to find Bill Moss waiting for them.

"My God, it's good to see you back in harness, boy," said Schenke. Moss had had a siege in the hospital, run down and nearly killed by some j.d.'s back in June. He was still looking a little pale, a little thinner than he had been, but he filled his uniform and his grip was firm.

"Thanks. My first night back on duty, matter of fact." He was teamed with an older uniformed man, Zimmerman. "And what do we come across but a body." He swung his flashlight.

"The car wasn't there first time we passed," said Zimmerman. "Call it an hour ago. Our lights just caught it when we came round from Flower—we thought it was a drunk till we looked."

They looked. It was a year-old Ford Mustang, and the body was slumped over the wheel. He was a big man, and there was a good deal of blood on the white vinyl upholstery. The driver's window was open; Conway reached in and felt the man's neck. "Barely cold," he said. "Shot or stabbed or what?" Then he spotted the knife, in the shifting flashlight beam: a short heavy hunting knife lying in the front passenger seat. "Do we call the lab, Bob?"

"Better have it towed in," said Schenke. "They'll be wild if we mess up any prints."

"Better safe than sorry," agreed Conway. They stood

58-

over the ambulance attendants to supervise the removal of the body, preserving possible evidence. When it was out on a stretcher Conway bent over it and said, "My God, Bob, it's a minister." The body, in the light of several flashlights, was revealed to be a rather handsome man, forty to fifty, clean-shaven, gray-haired, wearing a severely-cut black suit and a clerical collar.

With care, Conway bent, not touching anything, to peer in the open door of the Mustang. "They will still do it. We tell 'em to carry it in the glove compartment, but they don't listen." He manipulated his flashlight to bear on the registration-slip, clipped in its plastic envelope to the visor. "Evidently his own car. Reverend Adam Hatch, address on Los Feliz."

"What the hell?" said Schenke. "What was he doing down here?" They looked around. On this block of Olympic Boulevard there were mostly small shops, all closed now. The only place open was a little wine-and-beer tavern just up from the corner, its modest neon sign still lit, *Ted's Place.* "Any use to ask questions there?"

"Probably not, but we'd better."

The tow truck came and bore the Mustang away to the police garage. They went up to the tavern and asked questions. It was a small place, with only a few customers in on Sunday night: it looked like an ordinary neighborhood place. There was a three-piece combo, drums, piano and sax. The fat Irish bartender was also the owner, and he said, never any trouble, he got nice quiet types in, young working types from the neighborhood. The customers bore him out. There certainly hadn't been a minister in the place tonight.

The piano player pointed out that it was illegal to park on the street after nine P.M. on Sunday, on account of the street-sweeper. The combo had started playing at eight-thirty, all got here together, and there hadn't been any cars parked on the street then. "There's a lot on the side street."

The drummer, a thin dark fellow with a wisp of moustache, said he'd gone out in front "for a breath of air" when they took a break about ten o'clock, and there hadn't been any car parked on the street then. Everybody shook their heads at the description of the body.

"A minister, for God's sake," said Conway. Back at the office, they found the phone number matching the address and tried it, but got no answer. "So, leave it to the day watch."

------------------------- Four

"A minister, for God's sake!" said Hackett on Monday morning, looking at Conway's notes. It was Palliser's day off, but to balance that they had Henry Glasser back. He came in while Hackett was sharing Conway's notes with Higgins, and gravitated over to Wanda Larsen's desk; rumor had it that he was interested in that direction. Glasser was another hard plodder like Piggott, a good man. "Good vacation, Henry?"

"So-so. No money to go anywhere. What do we hear from Landers, he getting back next week?"

"Probably—unless they decide to take off for Tahiti." Conway had left the postcard on Hackett's desk. "And not that business has been exactly slow—if there's not much of anywhere to go on it—we've now got a minister stabbed to death."

"Well, most of them are human," said Glasser, deadpan.

"We'd better do some work on it," said Hackett. They now had, on the various heist-jobs, the first hopeful lead: that liquor store owner picking Buck Rainey's mug shot. There was a lineup arranged for nine o'clock. Higgins could cover that. The paperwork went on forever; Grace would be getting a couple of statements from the firemen, other occupants of that hellhole, about the dead body yesterday. At twenty past eight Chief Pomeroy of the Merced force came in with his witnesses, and Mendoza delayed routine a little by punctiliously introducing his senior sergeants. Pomeroy, who was a spare gray man with shrewd pale eyes in a tanned face, looked a little doubtfully at Mendoza's suave tailoring and gold cuff links. The two witnesses were ordinary-looking citizens, a little countrified.

"I've heard some stories about your artist fellows," said Pomeroy. "Be interesting to see what they might come up with. You got quite a setup here."

"We like it. If you'd like to look around, while the artist does his job, I can provide a guide," said Mendoza genially. He took them down to the lab himself.

The liquor store owner, Hansen, came in punctually, and Higgins and Glasser went with him to attend the lineup. Hackett said to Piggott, "You might have some ideas about how a minister comes to get murdered. We'd better find out who to break the news to anyway."

"What kind of minister was he?"

"That we'll find out too," said Hackett. "Let's go and have a look at him." Sometimes, not always, a corpse could be interesting: tell you something about what kind of person had inhabited it. They went over to the morgue, where an attendant told them the doctors were busy, two autopsies going on. "That's all right," said Hackett, "we just want to see that body fetched in last night."

"Oh, some kind of minister by the clothes," said the attendant. "He had on a Come-to-Jesus collar." Piggott looked disapproving. "We sent his clothes over to your lab."

Dressed in clerical habit, the Reverend Adam Hatch would have been impressive. He had been a tall, solid man, big-boned and carrying no fat, with a good deal of gray hair, a strong Roman nose, a clean-shaven square chin. He might have been any age between forty and fifty. Certainly he didn't look as if he'd belonged to some obscure sect, with one of those ministerial titles-by-mail.

The lab, of course, wouldn't have got to the clothes or the car yet. Hackett and Piggott went up to Hollywood in Hackett's scarlet Barracuda, to the address on Los Feliz. It was one of the older, very handsome apartment buildings, eight units, tan brick, and the Reverend Hatch was listed as occupying number two, at the right on the ground floor. "They couldn't raise anybody last night," said Hackett. "Could be he lived alone." But in a moment the door was opened by a slim good-looking colored woman in a neat cotton dress. She looked at the badge in dismay, she heard the news with astonished grief, she told them what a fine man the Reverend Hatch was. Her name was Enid Waters, she'd worked for the reverend twice a week for fourteen years, and he was the nicest gentleman she'd ever worked for.

"Killed!" she said. "How could he get killed? Murdered? Oh, my Lord, the things that happen nowadays—I just can't believe it! Well, at least if anybody ever went straight to heaven it was him—such a good man he was, everybody'll tell you." She could tell them that he'd been a bachelor, lived here alone; he had been pastor of the Christian Fellowship Church on Beverly Boulevard. He had a sister somewhere in Arizona, a Mrs. Goodley, she'd visited him here once last year.

"We'd like to look around here," said Hackett.

"Yes, sir, anything you say, though I don't know what you'd expect to find here to tell you who murdered him. Murder! It just don't seem possible, such a good man, a real godly man. I wasn't surprised he wasn't here this morning, I've got a key of course, because he'd be up and out to church or somewhere most mornings."

The apartment didn't tell them much except that Hatch had been a fastidious dresser if not flamboyant, very neat, not a keeper of miscellany. They found an address book, but there was nothing suggestive in it at first glance. They took down the sister's address; she'd have to be notified. There were a good many books, some nice old furniture well cared for, a modest stereo and a lot of classical records. There was a desk in the second bedroom, but evidently he hadn't kept his correspondence if he got much, and the only papers in the drawers were copies of sermons.

Enid Waters said he hardly ever entertained people at the apartment. "I can't recollect a party, even people for dinner, since I did for him. He was an awful quiet gentleman. Oh, when his sister was here that time she had some people in, but she did all the cooking herself. He fixed his own breakfast but he ate out a lot—one gentleman alone, I reckon it was easier for him."

Probably somebody at the church could identify the body officially: deacons, did they have those any more? Piggott said it depended on the church. It turned out to be a handsome one, fairly new, brick and synthetic stone and modeled after the Recessional church at Forest Lawn. It was open, and they found two people there: the assistant pastor, a David Mayse, and the organist, Miss Parker. They listened to more of the same from them, astonishment, grief, exclamations about all the violence around, the Reverend Hatch such a fine man.

"He was found in his car down on Olympic Boulevard," said Hackett. "Can you suggest any reason he might have been there, late in the evening?"

Mayse was a prissy little man with weak eyes behind

very thick lenses. He blinked rapidly. "Dear me, no. That is, well, dear me, I do just wonder—I really don't know, but I suppose it might have been something to do with his work at the clinic. He was very much concerned with young people, you know—so sad to see so many of them falling away from the church—he had instituted several programs here, to encourage them to come regularly. And he was very interested in this terrible drug problem, he was giving his time to this private clinic, counseling you know, the patients there—young people trying to—"

"Kick the habit," said Hackett. "What clinic was that?" Mayse gave him the name: a new one to Hackett, in West Hollywood.

"I believe he sometimes saw people on a private basis, if he felt he could help. It's all I could think of, but it doesn't seem— Most likely it was just some of this random violence we see so much of— Dear me, he will be sadly missed," said Mayse fretfully.

"Well," said Hackett, back in the car, "see what the clinic can tell us. But evidently he wasn't robbed, by what Conway said. Which may be neither here nor there. But he seems to have been a very upright character—"

"Candles on the altar," said Piggott. "And statues. But it does take all sorts. I'm not a betting man, Art, but it looks to me as if maybe Hatch was trying to reclaim one of his dopies who wasn't ready to get reclaimed. These clinics, aren't some of them like A.A.? You get the urge, call for help, they send somebody to hold your hand."

"Possible," said Hackett. "Let's go and ask."

At the lineup, Hansen identified Buck Rainey immediately and positively. "That's one of them. The one that held the gun on me. I'll swear that."

That was a step further on. Higgins and Glasser took

Rainey up to an interrogation room and started patiently leaning on him. It was the usual tiresome routine.

"It wasn't me. That guy's wrong, 's all. I never done that."

"Now, Rainey, you heard him identify you. If you weren't there last Wednesday night pulling that heist, where were you?"

"I don't just seem to remember, but I never done that."

"Come on, Buck, why not make it easy for yourself? Who was your pal?"

"I never done it. That guy's crazy."

It was all fairly stupid; this kind of day-to-day crime usually was. By what the witnesses said neither man had made any attempt at disguise, stocking masks or whatever; and Rainey at least was distinctive, big and burly with two cauliflower ears, a noticeable scar on one cheek.

"Come on and tell us about it. Where's the gun?"

"I didn't do nothin'."

"Come on, the man picked you right off. Tell us about it."

After forty minutes of sullen denial, Rainey said quite suddenly, "Oh, hell. You ain't gonna give up on it, damn you—I guess you gonna arrest me for it anyways, ain't you?"

"That's right," said Higgins. "The man said it was you."

"So why should I go to jail and him stay loose?" said Rainey, frowning. "I guess I tell you. It was Lee Stack with me."

"At the liquor store on Wednesday night."

"Yeah. Not as much bread as we figgered, neither— a lousy hunnerd bucks. We split it."

"Any idea where Stack hangs out?"

"Sure, man. He got a pad down near where I been livin', Hunnerd-fortieth. One o' the gov'ment apartments."

That was another step further on. They stashed him back in jail and queried R. and I. for any record on Stack. The package came up promptly; Stack had a record comparable to Rainey's, starting out with petty theft at age thirteen, progressing to B. and E., burglary, armed robbery and assault. He had got the usual slaps on the wrist, never served longer than two years.

Now having due cause, they asked Sergeant Lake to set up the machinery on an arrest warrant and search warrants, and went out to see if they could pick up Stack. At the ugly square pile of government housing they found Stack home. He opened the door to them, bottle in hand; he was already half drunk and at sight of the badge aimed a clumsy blow at Higgins with the bottle. Higgins said, "Goddamn!" as whiskey splattered all over his shirt, and grabbed Stack, reaching for the cuffs. But they had to call up a black-and-white to take him in, and by then various other tenants had appeared to start the name-calling and threats. The uniformed men waited around while Higgins and Glasser went through the two filthy rooms and came up with an old British Webley .45.

"My God," said Higgins, "I'd be scared to death to fire it—likely blow your hand off." It was covered with rust, a real antique. But faced with a gun the average citizen didn't tend to look close at its condition.

By the time they had broken for a hasty lunch and got back to the office, the arrest warrant had come through and a search warrant for Rainey's room. Sergeant Lake said there was an assistant D.A. with the boss, he didn't know what about.

"Whose toes have we been stepping on now?" wondered Higgins.

"The way you smell," said Lake, "somebody ought to investigate this corrupt force. I don't think it's anything serious—I heard him laughing a minute ago."

"That doesn't mean anything," said Glasser. "He isn't always feeling funny when he laughs."

Mendoza had, however, been genuinely amused, if cynically, for the moment. The assistant D.A., one of a battery of halfway bright young men to wear the title, was an eager beaver named Danvers, with political ambitions, and he was portentous and solemn.

"The warden thought it important enough to pass on to us, Lieutenant Mendoza. Folsom is a maximum-security institution. This Koutros has apparently been uttering threats for some time—apparently a number of the guards and other inmates as well have heard him swearing to, er, get you personally as soon as he got out. I expect you remember the case, I looked up the dossier and apparently—"

"Apparently!" said Mendoza. He had had to search his memory for Andreas Koutros, at that. He slid down on the end of his spine in his desk chair and looked at Danvers across the scattered cards on the desk. "Threatened men live long, so they say. *Chisme averiguada jamás es acabado*—no end to gossip."

"Well, the warden—and our office—thought you ought to know about the threats against you," said Danvers a little pettishly, "since the man is out. Just last week. Apparently he's continued to hold a grudge on you all these years—it doesn't seem very logical, but app—"

"Since when has human nature been logical?" Mendoza lit a new cigarette impatiently. He'd dredged the case, and Koutros, up from memory now: nearly sixteen years back, and he'd still been a sergeant, new in what was then the Homicide bureau. Koutros and his girl-friend, and what the hell had her name been?—Alicia,

Alicia Estaminez—had built a fairly crude little plot to get rid of Koutros' fat wife, and when they were dropped on and arrested, it happened to be Mendoza who'd done the arresting. There'd been charges of Murder One and conspiracy to commit Murder One, and a sentimental jury had acquitted Alicia: another jury gave Koutros life. Alicia had promptly killed herself with an overdose of sleeping tablets, and human nature being what it was, Koutros had fixed the blame on the officer who hunted him down. It had not, reflected Mendoza, been one of his more spectacular hunts, where his crystal ball had given him a hint about who was X: a very crude, unmysterious business altogether.

"We thought you should hear about it," said Danvers. "I needn't tell you that a prisoner serving a life term is technically eligible for parole in seven years, and the fact that Koutros has been denied parole until now apparently indicates that—"

"Oh, yes," said Mendoza sardonically. "Any safer to let him out in seven or fifteen years? Stakes down and wait for the throw! But I'm not peering over my shoulder for Koutros, Danvers."

"He'll have to report to a parole officer, of course. But he'll be living in this area—Hollywood. I talked to his officer, a Sergeant Reeder in Welfare and Rehabilitation. We only thought you'd like to know."

"So you've said seven times. ¡Gracias! I appreciate the concern, but I suspect Koutros will be too occupied enjoying life on the outside again—not that any prison is much of a punishment these days—to come hunting me on an old grudge."

"I'm sure I hope so," said Danvers stiffly.

Mendoza went out to lunch, to Federico's up on North Broadway, and ran into Grace; he told him about Koutros and Grace agreed with him. "Though you never know with these characters. People, they do come all sorts. I nearly went home for a bath after I'd visited what John called that hellhole again. How anybody can live like that—"

"Part of the new morality," said Mendoza.

"Which, as Matt would remind us, used to be called sin." Part of the turning away from any standards, moral or physical, but they were off base, Mendoza reflected, in calling it rebellion: it was just deliberate regression into uncivilization, if there was such a word.

When they got back to Parker Center, Mendoza dropped off at the lab wing to see if Pomeroy's witnesses and the artist had come up with anything. The two witnesses, Mr. and Mrs. Finley, looked tired but triumphant; Pomeroy and the artist, Garcia, were regarding a large black-and-white sketch interestedly. "Well, Lieutenant," said Pomeroy, looking up, "they say it's good. One of these jokers to a T, anyway."

"Oh, that's him," said Mrs. Finley confidently. "The other one, the smaller one, I couldn't be sure on exact descriptions, like nose and face shape and all—but that's the big one. It's not a face you'd forget so easy, even just seeing it once."

Mendoza rather agreed. The sketch, head and shoulders, showed a man in his early twenties, with a broad, high-cheekboned face narrowing to what might be a weak chin; the full beard, with the hint of curl, obscured the jawline, and the shoulder-length blond hair covered the ears, but it looked like a sketch of a real person; Garcia had caught a subtle hint of something furtive and violent —or was that just because he knew the subject was one of those who had left six bloody corpses behind him? Mendoza said suddenly, "Put one of those horned helmets on him, you've got an ancient Viking. That type."

Garcia grinned and nodded; Pomeroy squinted at it

and looked surprised. "I guess it's a pretty long chance you'd have a mug shot of him here, but we might have a look."

Mendoza shrugged. "No charge for that." He doubted it; all they had to say that the man hailed from somewhere around L.A. was that license-plate frame, and the car could have changed hands; they didn't know it was this man's car. But he took them down to R. and I. to look. The policewoman who came up was dark, not very pretty; he thought of pert blond Phil O'Neill—now Landers.

When he got back to his office Grace was talking with Hackett and Piggott. "You've got a couple of autopsy reports," said Sergeant Lake.

"So let's see if they offer us anything." Mendoza took them into his office, the other three after him. "Linda Norcott, results of further lab tests—nothing much we didn't know. Manual strangulation. She wasn't raped, no evidence of intercourse. Died between midnight and six A.M. last Tuesday."

"Of course," said Hackett, perching his bulk on the corner of the desk, "she must have known more men than the three we've heard about."

"*Ya lo creo*. Find some of her girl-friends and hope they can tell us about them. Or she could have picked up somebody on the street."

"Not much to go on, anyway."

"It's always seemed a little funny to me, speaking literally," said Piggott, "that the Bible calls them strange women. Anything but, you come to think."

Mendoza abandoned that and took up the other report. "Our Jane Doe on the freeway. Well, well. Macabre list of damages—she was smashed up well and good— both legs broken, internal injuries, ribs, one shoulder— direct cause of death, massive fracture to front of skull —I won't burden you with the medical terms—complicated by hemorrhage from injuries to the body. Complicated by! I should think she died the second she hit—and it was just luck she landed on the shoulder and didn't create a pile-up down there. And so we come to it—tests still in progress, but provisional opinion—and Bainbridge's provisional opinion is better than most medical conclusions—subject had ingested a considerable amount of marijuana into the bloodstream within one to two hours before death. *¡Cómo!* No alcohol present. And so on and so on. Mmhm. Description. We'll pass that on to Missing Persons in case she's listed somewhere, and somebody may have her prints, of course. Between eighteen and twenty-two—*¡caray,* these kids!—five-three, a hundred and ten, olive skin, black hair, brown eyes. Tattoos—*¡caramba! ¿Qué mono?* I will be damned, these idiotic kids—"

"Tattoos?" said Grace, interested.

"Mmhm. Upper left arm, *Beatrice May.* Lower left forearm, *Peace And Love.* Lower right forearm, *Stevie* in a heart, an Egyptian ankh, and—what the hell's this?—TITFDOTROYL. What the hell?"

"Say that again, slower," said Hackett. "What the hell indeed."

"Some organization—initials?" suggested Grace. "Some of these outfits have pretty outlandish names."

"Outlandish is the word," said Mendoza.

"Say it again," said Piggott. "TIT— Wait a minute." He got out his notebook and scribbled in it. "Well, it could be that. They go in for mottoes, seems like, and that's one of their favorites. I saw it on a bumper sticker just the other day. Tomorrow is the first day of the rest of your life."

"Oh. Unlike some others I've heard, incontestable logic," said Mendoza. "Nobody can deny that, Matt. To continue with the tattoos. Upper right arm, *Tommy.* Back of right hand, a so-called peace sign. Back of left hand, *Love* again. Talk about going back to the jungle."

"But all that should help to identify her," said Grace.

"We'll pass it on to Carey anyway."

"And you'd better hear about this minister," said Hackett.

"Wait till I've talked to Carey." But the description of Beatrice May—if that was Jane Doe's name—and her various decorations didn't ring a bell with Carey of Missing Persons. "What I have got," he told Mendoza, "just as of now, is a report that might tie up to one of your bodies. That hit-run victim. Man called in ten minutes ago and reported this Mrs. Adeline Fermin missing. She's a practical nurse, been on vacation, reason nobody missed her till now, I suppose. He's a Dr. Ferguson, convalescent home on Vermont."

"Women's work," said Mendoza. "*Bueno.*" He passed the address on to Grace. "So what about the minister, Art?"

Dr. Ferguson identified the body in the cold tray as Mrs. Adeline Fermin. He seemed to be a nice fellow, distressed and voluble. She'd worked at his convalescent home for twelve years, a very reliable efficient woman. She'd been on vacation for two weeks, due to come back to work today, but they'd already been worried about her because another of the nurses, Miss Spaulding, had been a great friend of hers and they'd arranged to meet for dinner and a show last Friday night, and when Mrs. Fermin didn't turn up—or for work today— He couldn't say why she hadn't been carrying any identification, it was a terrible thing, lying here all this time.

Grace was just sufficiently curious to see Miss Spaulding, who—told the location of the hit-run—burst into tears and said that was right up the block from Addie's apartment on Geneva Street and she'd most likely been going up to the drugstore and just took her change-purse with her.

They hadn't even a vague description of the car; they'd never get anybody for that one.

Higgins and Glasser got back to headquarters at four o'clock, after another round of talking to Rainey and Stack at the jail, and then on a couple of hours' hunt for more heisters. They were more than ready to call it a day, but Sergeant Lake had just had a call, and there was a report in from NCIC.

"So I'll pull rank on you," said Higgins, and took the report. Glasser said resignedly that age would tell on a man, and plodded out again. The new call was from a black-and-white, address on Virgil.

Higgins sat down at his desk with a paper cup of coffee from the machine down the hall and read the report. He had the random thought that they seemed to be hearing about a lot of other people's work these days. It could be something or nothing. It dated back. Last Friday a party of campers in the wilds of northern Utah had come on two badly injured men beside an old truck at a campsite. Identified as John Weston and Frederic Aldray, both of Provo, Utah, and known to be on a vacation trip —object, fishing, hiking, rabbit hunting. Brought to the nearest hospital, both men had been unconscious; doctors said, beaten and shot. Weston was still in a coma and not expected to recover, but Aldray had regained consciousness yesterday and told the police they had been attacked by two men they had befriended along the road. The men had hailed them for help with their car, and Aldray had managed to fix it up—he was an amateur mechanic. The men, who gave the names of Green and Thorson, had admitted they were "city fellows" and not used to camping, so Aldray and Weston had invited them to share a campsite. Green and Thorson, he said, must have attacked him and Weston when they were asleep that night, robbed them and presumably taken off in their car, since Weston's truck was still there.

He had given a description of the two men—early twenties, Thorson bigger than Green, with a beard—but a better one of their car. It was a 1960 Chrysler four-door sedan, light green; it had a dent in the left rear side, a broken front bumper, and the left rear window was cracked; and it was wearing California license plates, orange on black, and an old bumper sticker that said GO L.A. SHRINERS!

Green and Thorson—which were undoubtedly not their names—had got away with two good rifles, a Remington bolt-action 30-30 and an H. and R. .22, about fourteen dollars in cash, a pair of expensive binoculars and a brand-new telescopic sight. There wasn't a ballistics report as yet, but the assumption was that Weston and Aldray had been shot with one or both of the rifles.

Higgins sighed. The Shriners' amateur hockey team was certainly based in L.A., but how they could be expected to locate that car, with nothing else to go on—

Needle in a haystack, he thought. Barring the very long coincidence. California plates be damned, it could be anywhere, and the men anywhere else.

"I just don't know what I'm going to say to Jack," said Marion Hawley dully. "I just don't know. I never suspected Angie'd do a thing like that. This dope. I know some of the kids take it, the papers say it's all around, but I never thought Angie'd do like that. Just slum kids. Angie was a good girl. She never gave us any worry. I don't know what to say to Jack, he'll be wild. Just wild."

The address on Virgil was a shabby four-family apartment house. The black-and-white was still parked in front, the red Fire Department ambulance catered into the curb behind it. Upstairs, in the little second bedroom of the neatly-kept old apartment, was the body: a once-pretty dark girl about seventeen sprawled across the bed.

That TV program about the paramedics had made people aware of them. Mrs. Hawley hadn't put in the call: the resident manager, an efficient-looking elderly man named Galt, had done that. "I figured maybe they could still save her, oxygen or something." The paramedics offered the expert opinion that it was an O.D. of barbs; they had found a tube of red devils in her handbag beside the bed. She'd been dead about two hours.

"But how could it happen to Angie? I never suspected Angie'd have anything to do with that awful dope! I don't know how to tell Jack. I don't—"

"You'd never seen your daughter acting—oh, a little abnormal, strange?" asked Glasser. "Noticed her pupils dilated—any loss of appetite—slurred speech? Any unusual odor?"

She looked at him with bewildered eyes. "What?" she said. "I don't know what you mean. Kids now, they like to be independent, they don't like you to interfere, try to tell them what to do. I guess it's natural—I never liked my ma giving me orders—and Angie, she's nearly eighteen, grown up. She didn't like us telling her—I didn't so much take to that Andrews boy she's been dating, but I couldn't say anything, he wasn't any different than the rest of them, I guess, all the hair and funny sideburns—Jack, he's so proud of Angie being so popular with the boys—girls too, everybody likes Angie—"

Glasser felt tired. It really wasn't part of his job to help her explain to her husband that they'd cheated Angie: that the rules and regulations told the kids that somebody cared, and without them they were easy prey for the merchants of the new morality.

Galt said, "I can call your husband for you if you want, Mrs. Hawley."

"I just don't know what to say to him. He was so proud of her—"

Glasser went back to the office and told Wanda about it, to put in one of her efficiently typed reports. "I get tired," he said. "First day back off vacation, the old routine."

"The rat race. The heat wave doesn't help," said Wanda sympathetically.

"I thought maybe we could take a picnic lunch somewhere, some night," said Glasser. "Griffith Park?"

"It's full of the love children, Henry." She smiled up at him. "You can take me to dinner as soon as I've typed this—and we'll both have a drink first."

"Good deal," said Glasser, brightening.

Tuesday morning, the thermometer hit a hundred and three by eight o'clock. They didn't usually get it so hot in August.

It was Grace's day off, but everybody else was in by eight-fifteen. That Dosser was due to be arraigned this morning; Hackett would cover that. There would be a little legwork on the Hawley girl, to see if they could locate her supplier, but likely it would come to nothing: there were too many around.

Pomeroy's witnesses had, surprisingly, picked a mug shot out of the books: Theodore Podmore, record of B. and E., assault, statutory rape. Mendoza, coming in to hear that and look at the mug shot, was dubious. It didn't match the artist's sketch all that close; but there it was, they'd try to find him and ask some questions. Pomeroy and the witnesses had departed homeward to Merced.

-77

There was, of course, always the paperwork, reports to read. It was Mendoza's job to keep a finger on all the threads in the cases passing through their hands, to know the day-by-day status of what was going on. The thankless, never-ending, never-static job—he sometimes thought he stayed on it from inertia. At ten-fifteen he was reading the latest report Wanda had left on his desk when Hackett came in.

"This minister, Luis," said Hackett, perching on the corner of the desk. Sergeant Lake looked in the open door and said there was a citizen asking to see the boss.

"Or somebody important. A Mr. Clyde Goodfellow. He showed me his Social Security card, library card, membership card in Elks and Kiwanis, and gave me his minister's phone number. He's a salesman for Lovett Brothers, wholesale construction parts, and he's got something on his conscience."

"*¡Qué interesante!* Any hint about what?"

"Oh, yes," said Lake. "About the girl on the freeway."

"*¡Parece mentira!* Our Beatrice May, if she is. Shove him in, Jimmy." Lake went out, grinning, and in a moment Mr. Goodfellow came in hesitantly. He was about forty, plump, balding, conventionally dressed in a navy suit and white shirt, a rather gay red tie.

"Listen," he said plaintively before any amenities could be observed, "I didn't know! I never dreamed— Look, I hope I know better than to pick up hitchhikers on the road or even in town, fellows I mean, but this girl! She looked so young, I got a daughter myself, what these damn-fool kids think they're doing running all over—"

"Suppose you tell us about it from the beginning," said Mendoza, and the phone rang on his desk. "Sit down. . . . Yes, Jimmy?"

Sergeant Lake said tersely, "Your wife."

"Excuse me a moment. . . . *¿Enamorada?*"

"Luis!" said Alison in a great gulping sob. "Luis, the twins are gone! We think—we're afraid—because Mairí says—they've just vanished! And there was a man at the door—and Cedric barked—and they're simply *gone—*"

------------------------ **Five**

"Listen," said Mr. Goodfellow, looking at Hackett rather desperately, "I didn't want to get into any trouble—I know I shouldn't have done it, but all I could think of—how it'd look! A married man—and that girl! That fool girl! Look, I—it was such a surprise, who'd have expected a thing like that? I ask you? It was my wife said I've got to come and tell you about it, straight, just what happened. She says you'll give me a fair hearing, take things into account. The way it happened—is it all right if I smoke?"

"Sure," and Hackett offered him a cigarette. He was listening rather absently; what had got into Luis, rushing out like that—Alison on the phone, by his voice: something wrong at home? Accident— "You told Sergeant Lake this is about the girl on the freeway, last Friday?"

"My God," said Goodfellow. "My God. I just hope you'll believe me, Captain—"

"Sergeant Hackett."

"Sergeant. My God. Never had such an experience in my life, and catch me ever picking up a hitchhiker again! See, I've got to drive all over on my job, and I was out the

80-

other side of Norwalk Friday morning, around Ninety-nine Palms. This girl was standing right up from where I'd left the car, outside this contractor's office. She looked so damn young, innocent—these kids—the girls, it's a wonder they don't all end up raped and murdered, the characters around—and she asked me for a ride. I know I was a fool. Damn it, I felt sorry for her, Sergeant—I hope to God you'll believe me, that was all! She said she wanted to go to Santa Monica. Well, I was headed back downtown, I said I'd take her that far. Tell you one thing," said Goodfellow, who was perspiring even in the air conditioning, "it was a lesson to me another way. My God, these kids! Talk about free and easy! She said she'd hitched across country—she was from Bangor, Maine—"

"Did she tell you her name?"

"Sure, Beatrice Anderson. I tell you one thing, Sergeant, it sure opened my eyes—my little girl's only ten, but I'll sure be talking to her like a Dutch uncle about that, you better believe it! Listen, I've read a lot of stuff, newspapers and magazines, about the dope, but everybody says the marijuana isn't dangerous, not what they call addictive, just a little kick. My God." Goodfellow lit a new cigarette from the stub of his first, and Hackett thought about all the research that was turning up about marijuana. So many of the results once laid to LSD and heroin now linked to the harmless Mary Jane; but the research findings didn't get printed in places the public would see them. "She got out a pack of cigarettes, I offered her one of mine but she turned it down. She was—she laughed about it, said I ought to try one of hers—and there was a funny smell—I was, God forgive me, I was interested, I'd never—you know, the average citizen doesn't come in contact—I asked her what was so different about it, and she said it was, er, grass. Pot. Marijuana. I was, God forgive me, I believed what I'd read about it—"

"Just a little kick," said Hackett. "Yes."

"And she said that was right, she didn't go for the real dope, but the grass was nothing. *Had* she had anything else? I don't know, I just wondered. I hope you're believing me. I—we'd come back on the Golden State, to the Stack, and I'd just switched onto the Hollywood freeway when, my God, she starts screaming—oh, my God, Sergeant, the awful thing about it was, she was so happy! She was laughing like crazy, and bouncing around on the seat, and all of a sudden she started yelling, 'I'm gonna fly, I'm gonna fly'—and my God, before I knew what was happening she was out the door—"

"Euphoric," said Hackett.

"What?"

"The euphoric state. It's very common at a certain stage, with a lot of drugs. You weren't struggling with her?"

"Listen, if I'd known what she was going to do, I would have been, but there wasn't time—I was driving! I saw her start to go with the tail of my eye, as it were, and I jammed on the brake without thinking, I made a grab to try to pull her back, but—my God! I'd just turned to, you know, look at her—never thought of any traffic behind—just one split second—and she'd fallen against the cement wall, the guardrail you know, and before the damn car was stopped she climbed on top of it and *went*. My God. She thought she *could* fly, she put out her arms and I can see that damn backpack she had on kind of soaring over her head when she went over—Jesus!" said Goodfellow limply.

"Well, that clears up a bit," said Hackett. "We're very glad you came in, Mr. Goodfellow. Believe you? With what showed up at the autopsy, on the whole, yes. But you should have—"

"Stopped and reported it. Tell *me!*" said Goodfellow.

"I know, I know. But I was so shook—things like that just don't happen—I lost my head, I admit it. All I could think of, what it would look like—me a respectable married man. I knew she had to be killed, that drop. I was shook. I got out of there, and got off at the next ramp and went home. And my wife's been arguing at me ever since, I should come and explain to you. You do believe me? Will I get charged with anything?"

"You'll probably get a fine and suspended sentence for leaving the scene of an accident. A technicality," Hackett told him. "We'll want you to make a statement now, sir, and you'll have to testify at the inquest. There hasn't been a date set, maybe the end of the week."

"My God," said Goodfellow. "It's a relief to get it off my mind! Sure—a statement—anything you say." He'd have told it all over again; Hackett took him out to Wanda's desk and settled him down to make the statement. So this cleared up Beatrice; and while it was an arresting little tale (and one Mr. Goodfellow would be telling the rest of his life) it wasn't all that unusual, to cops who saw too much of the various effects of the various drugs.

Automatically clearing up the routine, he fired off a telex to the police in Bangor, Maine. If she had any family there, they'd have to be notified; whether they wanted to claim the body or not, they'd be asked to pay for the funeral.

"You know what's up with the boss, Jimmy?"

"Not a clue. That was his wife—she sounded upset, but I didn't listen in. You forgot about Dosser getting arraigned, Matt went to cover it."

"Oh, hell, I'm sorry." But the way Luis had looked— Hackett felt uneasy. He went back to Goodfellow and Wanda, to be sure everything relevant got into the statement, heard the story all over, thanked Goodfellow for coming in, told him he'd be informed about the inquest.

Palliser came in about then, at a quarter to twelve, with another of the possibles from the computer's list of heist-men, and Hackett looked at him resignedly. Even in a big and busy city detective office, not every face was a strange one; there were a lot of repeaters on any criminal list. This was one they had automatically thought of for any one of several of the heist-jobs, but until now they hadn't found him. Walter Ivy, his rap-sheet amounting to quite a package from little stuff to big. His latest two terms had been on counts of armed robbery, and he was just off parole two weeks ago.

"He said he's been on vacation," said Palliser sardonically, "over in Vegas. Reason we couldn't find him at home. His wife backs him up." But that said nothing; she had a record too.

"So let's see if we can get him to say any different," said Hackett. The damned routine—and from past experience with Walter he doubted they would; Walter was just slightly smarter than the average street-thug, and knew they hadn't anything definite on him or they'd have said so.

They took him to an interrogation room, and it went just as Hackett had expected; the monotonous denials, the usual loaded questions. Forty minutes later he and Palliser had just exchanged a glance, mutually agreeing to call it quits and let him go, when there was a single sharp rap at the door and Higgins looked in. "Art—see you?"

At the expression on his craggy face they both came out to the narrow corridor, and Hackett shut the door. "George? What's up?"

"Luis just called in. It's the twins—it could be a snatch. Not a sign of them since about nine-fifteen. Wilcox Street's been out hunting, and it looks as if there could have been a diversion set up to get Mrs. MacTaggart away—nothing definite, no note, but it's only been about three hours—"

"Oh, my God!" said Hackett and Palliser together.

"They've just called the Feds. You know how that'll go. Wait and see. And there could be other answers. Not nice ones."

"What does he want us to do?"

"Sit tight. We'll be getting news. Just keep fingers crossed," said Higgins. "If a ransom note turns up—"

Ollie came out to the street where Thor was waiting, leaning on the building, smoking a cigarette. He was feeling scared and confused.

He'd thought it was pretty smart of Thor to think about that, how the square guys kind of shied off anybody with long hair, the beard—and a place like this, all the marble floors and walls, mostly square guys— Do it nice and easy, they said. Ollie looked younger than he was, nobody'd be scared of him. Go ask for the guy, now they knew his name from yesterday, give him the story about accidentally hitting his car in the lot, be polite and say about insurance, and the guy would want to see the car and all, come right out, so they'd get him in their heap, Thor waiting right outside, and pass the bad news. It was a good idea. Thor had good ideas. But now it was all shot to hell, and Ollie was scared.

"Listen," he said. "Listen, he isn't there. He's away some place."

"Oh, damn it to hell, so he'll come back in a while, stupid," said Thor. "What did they say?"

"No, listen, I mean he's gone. He's gone some place for a week, on vacation."

"You stupid creep, he wouldn't go on a vacation all by himself without his old lady and—"

"Well, I can't help it," said Ollie humbly. "That's

what they said—the guy I asked. He's gone, he won't be back for a week. Thor, what the hell we gonna do now?"

Mendoza had used the siren on the Ferrari across town, cut it as he turned up Laurel Canyon. As he swerved into the drive he spotted the car in front of the house, and knew the men just getting out of it: Sergeant Barth and Detective Laird of Wilcox Street.

He might have known Alison and Mairí would keep their heads; they weren't showing hysteria. Alison leaned into his bracing arm; she was tense and pale, but making calm good sense. "We've been out looking for over an hour—we should have called you before. Now don't tell me children wander, Sergeant—" She looked at Barth straightly. "Don't try to tell Luis either. They're not four, and they don't—they never have. And the dog raised a fuss about the time they must have—nobody's seen them anywhere on the block, and we've looked."

"Just tell us what happened and when," said Mendoza.

"There's nothing much what or when," said Alison. "I was out at the market. The twins were in the yard, just as usual, and Mairí was doing the breakfast dishes. The doorbell—we don't *know* that has anything to do with it, but—"

"Now you'd best let me tell all that, *achara*," said Mrs. MacTaggart. Somehow they'd all moved into the big L-shaped living room, but nobody sat down. Mrs. MacTaggart was pale too, her blue eyes fearful but steady, her silver curls firmly in place, her voice sensible. "The chimes went, and the twins were right out there at the back of the yard when I went to answer the door. 'Twas a man said he'd a television to deliver, and I'd quite an argument with him that it wasn't expected here.

He kept saying this was the address he had, and wouldna take no for an answer. When I finally convinced him he was wrong, I shut the door and then I could hear Cedric barking out back—a terrible row he was raising—and when I looked, he was right at the back wall, reared up there, barking like a mad thing. And I went out, and the twins were gone. And—"

"And I got back just then," said Alison. "It couldn't have been five minutes all told, Luis—I saw that truck pull out of the drive as I came up."

"Any sign on it?" asked Barth.

"There was," said Mrs. MacTaggart. "B and G Deliveries, it said—not a very big truck, painted brown—"

"About the size of a telephone truck," said Alison. "Not that I noticed it especially, until Mairí— And so we started to look. They don't wander—oh, a few weeks back they did climb the fence a few times, but we cured them of that—"

"The back fence?" asked Barth.

"Yes—there's an alley runs through, but the next yard back was the attraction, there were some puppies— But they hadn't done that in weeks, honestly. And we *looked*. If they'd just wandered off a little way we'd have found— They're not four, they couldn't have got far, they'd have heard us calling—"

"Easy, *amada*," said Mendoza. "This delivery man, Mairí. No address on the truck?"

"There was not. Just B and G Deliveries. A scrawny body he was, a young fellow with a big nose and blondish hair."

"It seems to me we don't want to rush into anything here," said Barth, rubbing his chin. "Let's just be sure it's not the first time they've, um, gone adventuring. Kids of four—I've raised a couple of my own, you know."

"We've *looked*—they couldn't have got far. We've

been all up and down this block and the next, and they couldn't have got farther." These were long blocks here. Barth met Mendoza's eye and they shared, as cops, a mutual thought. These were also blocks of houses set back from the street, many with hedges screening front yards; and it was in the kind of neighborhood where few people did their own gardening and would be outside.

"Just not to jump to any conclusions," said Barth, "we'd better have another thorough look all around. Now, I know how you feel, Mrs. Mendoza. But we just want to be sure. I'll get some more men up here—where's the phone?"

Mendoza said gently, "Not uniformed men, Barth. Just in case." Barth looked at him and nodded once.

"Luis, you don't think—it was the first thing Mairí said, but I can't—you *don't?*" Alison turned her head into his shoulder.

"I don't think anything yet. As Barth says, we want to be sure."

Barth came back. "How are they dressed?"

"J-Johnny's wearing brown shorts and a yellow shirt, and Terry's in a blue and white plaid dress." Alison's voice shook. "She argued about it—it was a little wrinkled, and she's so d-darn persnickety—just like you, Luis—"

"Now, my lamb," said Mairí, "it could be we didna look far enough, there's always a first time as the man says, and they're venturesome childer goodness knows. It's just all the horrors you see in the papers, and us hearing more about them than most—likely we're just imagining something isn't so at all, and they'll find—" But she was frightened; her hands clasped together tightly.

"There's ground to cover up here," said Barth, "but we'll be thorough. Just to be sure."

Four more plainclothesmen came up from Wilcox Street to join the hunt. Laird, Mendoza and Barth went out to the back yard and Barth grunted, surveying it. "You've got two lots here? Big yard, and a lot of stuff to play with." Off to one side was the twins' slide, a big sandbox, the double swing. "But kids— What about the dog? Is he friendly? Would he go for a stranger in the yard?"

"Unlikely," said Mendoza. Cedric was down there by the back wall; he came when Mendoza called him, sniffed at the two strangers uninterestedly. "I think he might jump anybody who—tried to grab them, or hurt them." But Mrs. MacTaggart hadn't heard a sound from the twins.

"Well," said Barth doubtfully, "she last saw them down there. What about neighbors?"

"It's not the kind of neighborhood where people gossip over back fences," said Mendoza. They started down the yard.

"It doesn't look it. Nice to be rich," said Barth, and then closed his mouth tight.

It was nearly three hundred feet from the back porch, where three cats sat sunning themselves, to the end of the yard. There was a redwood-and-cement-block wall all round three sides of the back yard, nearly four feet high: but the ornamental cement blocks were open-faced, and both Cedric and the twins could see through. The shrubbery here was low planting, Mendoza didn't know what, not being a gardener, anonymous bushes, dark green and with no flowers now. There was no sign of any footprints in the dry packed earth, no marks on the wall. Cedric had come too, and uttered loud barks against the wall ten feet down. But there was nothing there either. Mendoza hoisted himself onto the wall, followed more slowly by the paunchy Barth.

"Anything?" asked Laird. Cedric barked again.

There was a little alley running straight behind the

lots here, dividing the house properties facing Rayo Grande from those facing opposite on the next street down. It was unpaved, about fifteen feet wide, and its bare earth was packed firm—in southern California, in August, there hadn't been a drop of rain in six months. Mendoza dropped over the wall, close in, and bent to look. If the twins or anybody else had passed this way, there was no sign; no prints would show here.

The yard across the alley was much trimmer, more manicured than the Mendozas' yard; it ran up in a green lawn, with neat flower beds at each side, to a paved patio partly sheltered by a green aluminum awning jutting out from a long wing of the house. The house was part brick, part redwood; it was newer than the Mendoza's house; the next street down, Laurelton Place, had only been subdivided and built on about two years ago.

"Know the people there?"

Mendoza shook his head. "But if anybody was out in any yard along here, they could have seen them." There was a low white-painted brick wall at the end of that yard; they stepped over it and started up to the house. These lots were wide, but this house was built on just one lot, and the next-door yard was close. As they came into the paved patio, they saw a woman out in the yard next door, a fat middle-aged woman in a sleeveless cotton dress, watering flower beds with a green hose. She looked at them in curiosity and alarm, strangers.

"Excuse me," said Mendoza, "we're looking for—two children who may have got out of their—my yard—across there. Have you seen—"

"Oh. No, I haven't seen any children. I only came out a few minutes ago, since Jim's retired we don't get up so early. You gave me a start, I must say. Some children lost? —I'm sorry."

"Do you know who lives here? If they—" Barth looked at the house. Its rear windows looked blank, one of them this side showing café curtains to mark it as kitchen or breakfast room. No one had come out to confront the trespassers.

"Oh, yes the Orrins, but they're away—off on vacation. I saw them drive off early last Friday."

"*¡Condenación!*" said Mendoza softly. "Thanks very much." They climbed back over the wall and went on up the alley. Nobody else was out in any yard, and in none of those they passed was there any cover either side, any dense shrubbery or trees; all lay open and empty; property up here was too recently built on to exhibit old, tall growths of anything.

The other men were covering Rayo Grande, Laurelton Place, the cross streets. In the five years since the Mendoza house had been built, many homes had gone up in the area; there were houses, people, all about, places to ask about two four-year-olds seen or not seen. But—

By twelve-thirty they were back at the house on Rayo Grande. The twins were nowhere within six blocks, and nobody had seen them. "It's a terrible thing to be saying," said Mairí, "but just the moment's relief, maybe. All I could be thinking, one of these men—"

"Luis?" Alison took a fierce grip on his arm.

Mendoza sat down and lit his tenth cigarette in an hour. "The delivery truck," he said to Barth. "It could have been a diversion. If they saw Alison drive off."

"Now wait a minute," said Barth. "You're a cop, Mendoza. Even movie stars get their addresses listed somewhere, but—"

"*Conforme.* There's a solution to every problem."

"You want to call the Feds?"

"Maybe we should have an hour ago."

The three FBI men who came were Valenti, Warren and Slaughter. Detachedly, Mendoza was aware that they were slightly relieved not to be dealing with the average muddleheaded citizen, but a cop; they could take short-cuts, use the common slang.

"The truck could have been a diversion," said Warren. He reminded Mendoza of Higgins, big and craggy-faced. Slaughter was tall and gangling, Valenti slim and dark and quick. "Valenti mentioned all your loot—just how common knowledge is it? You holding down a desk at headquarters?"

Mendoza shrugged. "*¿Por qué no?* It's never been a secret, all I can say. But what I'm thinking about now is last Friday's *Times*. I didn't take much notice at the time, but some enterprising reporter trying to liven up a story invented a nickname for me. I don't know if you saw it."

"The Gebhart hearing," said Valenti. "I saw it. So anybody who saw it too knows about your money."

"Goddamn it," said Mendoza, "there are a thousand richer men, more obvious targets—but—"

"But, anybody the wrong side of the line might be damned pleased to get money out of a cop—and also—" Slaughter looked at Alison and shut up.

"*¡No lo niego!*" said Mendoza violently. "That's the hell of it—I was annoyed about that damn-fool story, but it wasn't until just now—"

"And just how would any outside citizen, which-ever side of the line, know where you live?" said Warren. "Every cop lives in tight security—there's never a phone or a home address listed anywhere the public could get it. With good reason. I heard something about what happened in Detroit last year when those records got lifted from headquarters—anonymous calls, threats, bomb scares, cops and their wives assaulted, burglarized, God knows what." He looked at Alison and Mairí speculatively.

Mendoza laughed without mirth. "*Se.* You needn't worry about these two—cops' wives and families are aware of some facts of life. Tight security hell, Warren.

Parker Center's all over postcards you can buy for a dime. I have, for my sins, had my picture in the *Times* on occasion. And on the other hand, if somebody who looked reasonably honest wandered into headquarters and up to Robbery-Homicide, I could be spotted easy enough—there are people in and out, it's a busy office, and my name on my office door. Just use a little patience, sooner or later I come out and climb in the Ferrari at the end of a day, and when I'm not expecting a tail—"

"All right. It's just possible," said Warren. "We've got to play it that way, anyway. Just in case. Now I don't want to upset your wife, but we've got to get this straight. With kids this young, and the circumstances, it can be a snatch—but it can also be something else, the pervert. You know how that goes—everybody's mobile these days. They could have been picked up in a car—all right, you looked and asked, nobody could say if there'd been a car down that alley this morning, that doesn't say there wasn't—I have to say it. They could have been taken miles away, they could be—"

"All right," said Alison, sitting up straight. "I know that. I know it. But you've got to—take it all into account. In case it's something else."

"That's right." Warren looked at Mendoza. "You know what we'll be doing. I don't see any way on God's earth anybody could know your private phone number, but we've got to play both ends against the middle here. We'll put a tap and recorder on your phone here, and a man here round the clock, until we know. I think it's the hell of a lot likelier that if somebody wants to contact you it'll be at your office—easier to reach you there—so we'll put a tap on that phone too, and a man there. Thank God all your men are pros too, they'll know what to do, how to act."

"You needn't spell it out," said Mendoza tautly.

-93

"There used to be a few rules, even to pro crime. Anything goes now. There could be a ransom demand tonight or tomorrow or never. If it isn't the other thing. We wait and see."

"That's about the size of it," said Slaughter. "All we can do is wait. And if it is—something else, you know as well as I do it'll—come to light."

"To light," said Mendoza. Let there be light. Funny about words. He remembered the case they'd had just a while ago, the rape-killer, and the pathetic little body found up in Elysian Park, and the man they'd got for it— a lout of a man, now tucked away at Atascadero with the criminally insane. But was there any choice among evils? There used to be rules—a long time ago—the ransom paid, the hostage returned. These days, with too many of the wild ones running loose, no rules.

Johnny and Terry were nearly four—articulate, bright, smart kids; they could read. They could tell who had had them, when, and how. Even with the loot picked up— even now when the courts had all but outlawed the death penalty—especially now, when there wasn't that deterrent to casual murder of any degree—

He looked down at Alison and saw all that knowledge in her hazel-green eyes, Johnny's eyes. Terry looked like him: she had his grandmother's bright brown eyes and warm olive skin; but Johnny had his mother's eyes. "*Cara*," he said, "you're all right now. We don't know about this— we can't know yet."

"I'm all right, Luis," she said steadily. "I know. No point having hysterics. We—just wait. And we'll do what we have to do."

"That's my girl."

The Feds had been out in the hall, at the phone. Mairí had slipped away; when Warren came back he looked around and said, "Excuse me, Mrs. Mendoza—your maid or nurse or whatever you call her—are you quite sure she's trustworthy? How long have you had her? Does she live in?"

"Oh, don't be ridiculous," said Alison tiredly. She looked disheveled and a little wild, her red hair in a tangle where she'd run fingers through it, all her lipstick chewed off. "Mairí's like a grandmother to them. A friend— what we'd do without—she's been with them since they were babies. That's silly."

"That's the story, Art," said Mendoza on the phone. "You can expect the Feds. I don't need to spell it out."

"My God, Luis. No. You know what we're all feeling, boy. What Angel—and Mary—No, you needn't spell it. It's up in the air. Until we know something more." Hackett was remembering that body in Elysian Park too.

"There's no B and G Deliveries listed in any phone book," said Mendoza. "Does that change the odds? There hasn't been a new one out since March, but the phone company hasn't got a record of any B and G Deliveries. The Feds don't want any incoming calls here—we're leaving it open. I don't see how anybody could get hold of that number, but anything's possible. They're putting in another phone—I'll let you know the number in an hour. If anything shows—note, phone call—the Feds will pass it on. But it could be a while, even if—"

"Even if," said Hackett. "Are you thinking it could go back to that damn fool story in the *Times?* I don't see— My sweet Jesus!" said Hackett suddenly. "Oh, my good God—"

"¿Cómo dice?"

"Arnold Berry!" said Hackett loudly. "Berry! When he came in the other day—how he said he hoped you'd lose your— Am I exercising my imagination? It just hit me—Luis?"

-95

"That could be reaching for a very wild card," said Mendoza. "Yes. I don't think we'll tell the Feds about Berry right away, Arturo."

"*¿De veras?* You'd already thought about him," said Hackett. "What's in your mind, *hermano?*"

"They're very efficient boys," said Mendoza, "as a rule. But they will go by the book. They tell me to face realities, and also to wait and see if there's a ransom demand. *¿Y pues?* I said, damn the story in the *Times*, there are the hell of a lot richer men more obviously loaded and vulnerable. What does two and two add to—and are the odds really on a snatch?"

"*No sé,*" said Hackett. "I get you. What do you want?"

"We've got a little time on hand—I think. There's no need to tell the Feds about Berry right now. You go and find him, my Arturo. Go and talk to him—if you find him."

"We'll be on it," said Hackett tersely. "I read you. There's two possibilities—and maybe three. My God, Luis, there's nothing to say—"

"*Comprendo.* I'll be in touch. I may be a little trammeled here by these Feds."

"Let me have the new number as soon as you know. We'll all be holding good thoughts. *Hasta más tarde.*"

"*Hasta luego,*" said Mendoza.

Hackett had been sitting at Mendoza's desk; he went out to the big communal sergeants' office and found them all there, looking grim and as he came in expectant. He passed on all that. Somebody had called Grace and he'd come in, day off or no.

"What's the odds?" said Higgins angrily. "For God's sake, Art! The *Times* story, that's a nice expensive neighborhood, somebody could have tailed him home—how Goddamn likely is it? For Christ's sake, we all know that what it looks like is usually just what it is! And what this looks like we all know—the nut, the pervert. Like God knows how many nuts running around—"

"Two of them, George?" said Hackett. "Two active, lively kids nearly four? When there wasn't a peep out of either of them? A boy and a girl?"

"The nuts come all shapes and sizes. I think a snatch is a little way out. But this Berry—I can see that, all right. Let's go look for him." Palliser muttered profane agreement.

"And I can offer another little idea," said Grace. "I can indeed." He was leaning back in his desk chair, smoking; even on his day off he was dapper in gray suit and white shirt. His eyes were angry, if his voice was soft and casual. Grace liked kids. It had been a joke in the office, all his snapshots of the baby—the baby his wife couldn't have. They'd argued at the County Adoption Agency for six months before they got plump brown Celia Anne. "I don't know whether the rest of you heard about it—he was telling me yesterday. What that assistant D.A. came to see him about. This Koutros."

They listened to that, Higgins muttering cuss-words, and Hackett said, "By God, Jase. It's something else to think about. Luis's being deviled by these Feds, he had thought about Berry, but—Koutros is on P.A.?"

"Welfare and Rehab'll know his officer," said Higgins. "We'll talk to him. Just in case, my God— You said, two possibilities and maybe three." He looked savage, massaging his prognathous jaw.

"And what does it say in Holy Writ?" said Grace softly. "Vengeance belongs to the Lord. But people, they do come all sorts."

"There's another quote, Jase," said Piggott heavily. " 'Lo, I have made men upright; but they have sought out many inventions.' "

Wanda Larsen had been listening, sober and scared. "I'm sorry," she said in a small voice now, "but I don't believe in a kidnapper or this Berry or the Koutros man. It's—too complicated. Things aren't. I'm afraid Sergeant Higgins is right—it's the nut, just picking them up, poor darlings—and the lieutenant marrying so late, I've never met his wife but you all said how pretty she is and—it's so terrible but I just can't think it's anything else." She started to cry silently and Glasser mutely offered her his handkerchief.

"What the hell are we sitting talking for?" demanded Higgins belligerently. "It's something to do—find out for sure if there's anything to this, while the damn Feds wait for a ransom note!" He shut up as a man came past Sergeant Lake, who'd been listening silently.

"Warren, FBI," said the newcomer.

"We've been expecting you," said Hackett politely.

"Darling Phil," said Landers, "I suppose we ought to leave tomorrow."

"Um," said Phil. "I suppose." She wriggled her bare toes in the sand. "Sue'll be mad if we don't stop to see her and Jim. And we can go on down to Fresno on Thursday or Friday, and home Sunday."

Landers kissed her. They had the beach to themselves, there was nobody to see. They were going to live in Phil's apartment for a while: maybe start a family next year.

"Only," said Phil, "the paper says there's a heat wave going on down there, Tom. Let's cut across and drive down the coast road. Back to the rat race Monday—and thank heaven headquarters is air-conditioned."

------------------------------- Six

Hackett had found Sergeant Reeder, over at the Welfare and Rehabilitation bureau, just about ready to leave his office. Reeder looked surprised at the question, but took Hackett back into his office and looked up his file on Andreas Koutros.

"Something up?" he said alertly, eyeing Hackett. He looked as much of a tough cop as George Higgins, though he was just in the administrative side.

"Something," said Hackett shortly, "maybe. What do you think about this guy? The threats mean anything?"

"I don't know him well enough to say," said Reeder. "Sure, I'm his P.A. officer. You know the case load we're all carrying. Yeah, Folsom passed that on, about Koutros uttering threats. Nine times out of ten that kind of thing is just talk. He's never said anything out of line to me, but of course I've only seen him, what, three, four times."

"Where is he living, and doing what?"

"We got him a job as orderly at the French Hospital. He's a kind of queer customer, Hackett, a loner. But the board thought he was O.K. for parole. What the hell's this about?"

"On the q.t. for right now, maybe nothing. Has he got a room—an apartment?"

"A room, in a boarding house about six blocks from the hospital. Why? You think he's up to something? It's my job to know if he is."

Hackett just shook his head. "If he is, we'll let you know. What hours is he working, do you know?"

"Three to eleven P.M. shift."

The hackles lifted a little on Hackett's neck at that: Koutros would be free all morning. He got away from Reeder and drove over to the French Hospital, where the badge got him in to the personnel director, also about to leave for the day. He was received with some coolness, but got the answers to questions. Koutros had come on duty at his regular time, three that afternoon; his work had been satisfactory so far; yes, they knew he was on parole. Did the Sergeant want to see him?

There wasn't any point in trying to question him here. Hackett looked at Koutros from a little distance—a heavy-shouldered, dark man with a mop of dark hair streaked with gray, trundling a hospital-cart down the hall. This business of his hours left it all up in the air.

He called Angel from the office. There wasn't anything to tell her but the bald fact. She sounded tense, said Alison had called to give her the new number. "Art—there's just nothing to say. You don't know anything yet?"

"Not yet. I don't know when I'll get home, I'll pick up something." He went out for a hamburger; when he came back Higgins was there, with Palliser.

"I don't know what you think about Koutros, Art," said Higgins, "but we might have rung a loud bell with Arnold Berry. I like it and I don't like it. He's been living in a cheap apartment over by MacArthur Park, and regular

100-

on his job—up to last Thursday. I caught the head of the men's department at Bullock's. They haven't seen Berry since last Thursday and he hasn't called in sick or been in touch. At the apartment, there's a motherly widow across the hall who took an interest in him, knew about the fire and his family, and she says he's been brooding about it all over again, since a judge let Riley off so light. She's tried to cheer Berry up, fix him nice meals, she said, but he wouldn't talk to her or let her in since last Sunday —she's been keeping an eye out, you gather. And yesterday morning she saw him drive away in his old car and he hasn't been back."

"Yesterday morning," said Palliser. His long dark, not unhandsome face looked grave, a little sad. "It could tie in. He wouldn't try to keep the kids in an apartment."

"Keep them?" said Higgins savagely. "If Berry's behind this, he isn't thinking about ransom, John! So, maybe he just got fed up with his motherly neighbor and her potato salad, maybe he's just taken off blind, but it could say something. I made the car from D.M.V. Should we put out an A.P.B. on him?"

"Let's see what Luis says." Hackett dialed the new, second number at the house on Rayo Grande. He surmised there was a Fed listening to Mendoza's end of the conversation, which was monosyllabic. "What do you want to do, or can you say?"

"That's about it," said Mendoza. "He might tell us something interesting about the case if you can locate him."

"You want an A.P.B. out?"

"Conforme. As soon as you like."

"O.K. I think so too. Nothing yet?"

"Nada."

"Well—see you, boy." Hackett put down the phone. "He says yes. Where's the D.M.V. report?" The car was an old two-door Ford; they put an A.P.B. out on both car and Arnold Berry. The night watch came on, to hear about the twins for the first time; they said all the expectable things.

"God," said Conway, "it makes you hope it is a snatch. Hell of a thing to say, but the chances might be just a little better of getting them back. What are the odds?"

"Anybody's guess," said Higgins. "And there's a Fed sitting in his office. You can keep it to yourselves about Berry. But if any smell of him turns up, let us know *pronto.*"

"That's for sure. But if he's been gone since Monday he could be anywhere."

"Or holed up right here somewhere," said Palliser.

Before they left, a telex came in from a sergeant on the Bangor, Maine, force. Beatrice May Anderson's mother was still living there, and would claim the body, pay for the funeral. "Save the city a little money," said Hackett.

He went home to Angel. The kids were in bed. Safe in bed.

And Angel said, "When I think how Alison must be feeling—I'm glad we're not rich, Art. Not terribly rich."

"I guess right now, compared to Luis and Alison, we're rich, my Angel," said Hackett.

All the clocks seemed to have stopped working, Mendoza thought. Time slowed down. The Feds had been very quiet and efficient, no fuss to show, only the three men in business suits visible to neighbors, and one staying. The telephone truck—anybody might have phone trouble. And if anybody asked, they told Alison and Mairí, after the open hunt this morning, they were to say yes, the children were all right.

"We play it close to the chest," said Valenti with a humorless smile. "Time was, we could tell the press to clam up, keep a story under wraps if it might endanger somebody, and they'd cooperate like gentlemen. These days, we take no chances." He was installed beside the phone in the hall; he thanked Mairí politely at the offer of a tray.

He was the only one who made any pretense of eating. The house seemed larger than usual because it was so quiet. About nine o'clock Mendoza, going down the hall, discovered Mairí sitting in the dark in the twins' room, with her rosary in her lap. There was a full moon, and it touched her silver curls faintly.

"All this waiting about," she said. "All we can do is some special praying about it. God's been verra good to answer my prayers before now. I'll be out to early Mass."

It was a long time since he'd believed in any of that.

"And I do not care, Luis," said Alison miserably when he'd persuaded her to go to bed, "it's as much our own fault as anybody else's. Practice what we preach, and cops' kids taught to be so smart and careful! When have we ever warned them—about strange cars, strange people, taking presents? They're so little—they're never alone, somebody always with them, and I just never thought—I did think, later on, when they start nursery school, they ought to know more children, and they're going next month—all enrolled in the private one—but I've never said one word about all that! Johnny so friendly with everybody! Terry trusting anybody she meets! We should have had more sense—"

And hadn't he said it himself. Time sliding by, and parents, even the ones who meant to be sensible— Just yesterday they were babies, and he had never thought of that either. The twins always supervised, somebody knowing always where they were.

Where were they? Where, tonight, under a full moon?

The four cats were coiled as usual at the foot of the

bed, Bast washing Sheba and El Señor annoyed at the
disturbance, lashing his tail. Alison refused to take a sleeping pill.

He went down the hall, glancing at Valenti beside
the phone. Valenti, at ease in the upholstered chair moved
there, looked placidly ready to stay in the same position
all night.

Nobody could have that phone number. Nobody—
outside.

And Cedric was barking again.

Mendoza went out the back door. In the full moon-
light the yard looked very big and very empty. There was
the tall slide, the sandbox, the swings; an old toy airplane
of Johnny's lay by the back step. Under the moon, their
shaggy dog Cedric was down there at the end of the
yard, reared up against the wall, barking.

He had seen them go; but he didn't speak English.

Mendoza went back to Alison. He didn't think either
of them would sleep much.

Wednesday was supposed to be Glasser's day off, but
he came in. They all got in early. Nothing had showed;
Mendoza called in at eight to report that.

The A.P.B. hadn't turned up Arnold Berry yet. There
was a routine call from the coroner's office: the inquest on
Linda Norcott was set for tomorrow morning. The Fed
who'd been sitting at Mendoza's desk phone left when
another one came on at eight-fifteen.

Hackett looked around. "I don't know who'd like to
go with me to play-act at Koutros. All unofficial. If we
can scare him a little we might get a better idea if he fits
into this."

"I don't think so, Art—I hope to hell not," said Higgins, "but I'll go. You said he doesn't go to work until
three, he'd have had time. To— Does he have a car?"

"That's the one catch. No. That is, not that Reeder

knows. He's only been out two weeks, but he could have —no D.M.V. record but there are ways—"

"I wish to God we could turn up Berry," said Higgins. They went out together, the two big men, and Palliser lit another cigarette.

"Is there any fixed rule about it—how long you have to wait for a ransom note?"

"There won't be one," said Glasser. "It was the nut. A cop's kids, we say, would know better than go up to a stranger—but kids that young? If you ask me, it was the nut—just passing along that alley, or marking them before. They could be anywhere, dead or not." His voice was flat. "Higgins is right—what it looks like is usually just what it is. We don't get the complications."

"Satan never was very complicated," said Piggott. Grace had gone down the hall for another cup of coffee, and as he came back Sergeant Lake collided with him in the door and spilled it all over his jacket. Lake was towing a surprised-looking uniformed postman with one hand.

"Here it is! It's got to be! Get that Fed—it's a special delivery for the boss, and it's got to be—from the look of it—" He had the thing balanced carefully on one palm, and as Piggott ran for Mendoza's office he laid it carefully in the middle of Hackett's desk. The Fed, Slaughter, came bouncing in.

"Where is it? Who's touched it? Can I get an outside line on this phone?"

"It's a regular special delivery," said Glasser, peering at it.

"What the hell is this?" asked the postman. "Of course it's a regular—my first stop of the day, I just came from the Terminal Annex—what the hell?"

"All right," said Slaughter. "All right." He had Valenti on the phone, then Mendoza. "That was never mailed over a counter." They looked at it.

It was a cheap dime-store envelope, business size. It

was addressed in staggering print, ordinary ballpoint. LIET MENDOZA LAPD HEADQARTERS 150 L.A. ST. SPECAIL DELIVRY, and it bore a lot of stamps of different value—too many, adding up to nearly a dollar's worth, twenty or thirty cents too much for local special delivery. At one glance, without asking the postman, they knew that nobody at any local post office was going to remember taking that over the counter. It had probably been dropped into the local white-star box at the Terminal Annex some time last night; that was the postmark; and sorted out when the first shift came on. The postman, consulted, agreed with that. What else it might tell them remained to be seen.

"For God's sake, waste time calling your own office when you've got the world's top lab three floors up?" said Palliser. By the time Mendoza, Warren and Valenti walked in Duke had come to dust the envelope, and reported that there were no liftable latents on it. He had taken the postman's for comparison in case, but there was nothing doing. They let the postman go.

Mendoza picked up the envelope. He looked washed-out and rather pale this morning, but was precisely dressed as ever, silver-gray Dacron suit, white shirt, dark tie; he laid the perennial black homburg beside the phone on Hackett's desk. He slit the envelope on three sides and gently prodded the contents out with the letter-opener; Palliser silently used his pen to help unfold it and hold it flat.

It was a half sheet torn from a ruled tablet, and the same staggered printing ran down it. Mendoza said softly, "¡Válgame Dios!"

10 Gs in loker Un stat today 3 ocloc leve key in lok will be wachin & leve note tell abot kid.

"Ten G's?" said Warren blankly. "Ten? What the hell is this? Let's get this dusted!"

There were no useful latents on the note; just

smudges. The paper would be unidentifiable, the kind available at ten thousand stores.

"I don't like it," said Slaughter. "Ten G's? It could be a teaser."

"We have to play it," said Warren.

"Don't give me orders, *hermano*," said Mendoza. "I've dealt with the ones on the wrong side so long I've given up trying to classify them into types. So that latest snatch back east, the ransom was half a million—so this boy is behind the times, or feeling modest. We'll have to play the hand."

"It's the hell of a long chance," said Warren. "I say it's a teaser. But he's either a fool or an amateur to pick that spot, a locker at the Union Station. Tie a tail to him—"

"If you've got that good a tail," said Mendoza, "not to spook him."

"We've got one." Warren looked at his watch. "You can raise the loot right away? It may take you a little time —and that's another reason I don't like this, I don't think it's for real, he doesn't say a damn thing about small bills or whatever. It's a try-on—but it may give us a lead."

"I'll get the loot. Just be damned sure it's a smart tail." Mendoza met Palliser's eyes across the desk; his expression was sardonic, and Palliser realized he hadn't asked for Hackett or Higgins. He had probably had an educated guess where they'd be.

And into the little silence, all the men crowded in a tight little group there over the desk, Sergeant Lake among them, a woman's voice sounded hesitantly.

"Excuse me—they told me downstairs to come up here. It's about my brother, the police in Phoenix told me and I just got here. I'm Margaret Goodley. Is this where I'm supposed to come?"

As if at a signal the group broke formation. Mendoza marched out with Warren after him; Slaughter picked up the phone again. Sergeant Lake started back for the switchboard. Grace and Piggott drifted to their own desks, and Glasser out toward Wanda's. Palliser straightened. Over the years, the discipline of strict routine in a busy detective office had conditioned him, like any cop, to switch from case to case, automatically shift his mind to marshal remembered facts.

"Yes, Mrs. Goodley. I'm Sergeant Palliser. Would you like to sit down here? The Phoenix police explained to you about how your brother—?"

She nodded. She was a little plump woman about fifty, and she didn't look so much grieved as bewildered. "I can't understand how it could have happened. Adam lived such a quiet life—he hadn't many interests outside the church, I don't think. But all the violence in any big city—"

As Palliser explained about the mandatory autopsy, that she could claim the body after the inquest, he reflected on what Hackett and Piggott had turned up on the Reverend Hatch, which wasn't much. That one might go into Pending in the end. It had turned out that Hatch merely conducted a religious counseling class at the drug clinic, and few of the outpatients there had been interested; the idea that he could have been seeing any patients privately was a dud. It would have looked like the all-too-common assault for theft, some thug jumping him down there, except for the fact that he hadn't been robbed. He'd had forty dollars on him; and he had been in his car.

Mrs. Goodley couldn't tell them anything useful; she and her brother hadn't been close, she was a widow with her own interests over in Phoenix, and Hatch hadn't written her often. She knew next to nothing about his associates here.

When he'd seen her out, Palliser started over to kick this ransom note around with Grace, but the phone rang on Hackett's desk and he picked it up. "Jimmy?"

"I've got that Chief Pomeroy asking for the boss. You talk to him?"

"Put him on. Lieutenant Mendoza's out of the office, Chief. Palliser—will I do? You have something for us?"

"Not exactly," said Pomeroy's elderly voice. "But I thought I'd pass it on, Sergeant. On my way home yesterday—the Finleys drove their own car—I stopped in Chowchilla to see an old friend o' mine, chief of the force there, Dick Van Vorst. He was telling me they had a break-in there last Friday night that could sort of tie in with this bunch I'm after. Don't often have much happening, place like that. Pharmacist held up, knocked around some, and cash and drugs taken—barbiturates mostly. The description was kind of vague, but it could've been the same two men."

"Oh," said Palliser, wondering why Pomeroy should think they'd be interested.

"Point is," said Pomeroy, "if it was them, they were headed south from Merced. Just thought I'd mention it. Of course Chowchilla isn't right next door to you, but it's on the state highway heading for L.A."

"Oh," said Palliser again. "So it is. That could tie in. Thanks."

The phone shrilled on Grace's desk and he picked it up. As Palliser put his phone down, Grace was on his feet.

"Somebody's got to mind the store, John. New one—man shot on the street, Beverly and Hillhurst."

All the violence, Palliser thought. Tell any cop.

"And what about that ransom note?" said Grace in the Rambler. "I don't like to agree with Henry."

"No. However funny it may look, to the Feds or to us, that makes it definite, Jase—it is a snatch."

"I've got a queer feeling about it," said Grace, and was silent the rest of the way.

Somebody had to mind the store, and it was seldom

a day went by without something new showing up to work. They just hoped this one wouldn't make too much legwork. The heat wave was still with them.

It was, at first glance, something offbeat, which was exasperating. The ambulance was just leaving as Palliser slid the Rambler into the red-painted zone at the curb; the uniformed men in the black-and-white gave them the gist of what had happened.

"We thought it was a heist, when we saw it was a bank, but it wasn't. The guard hailed us, we'd just turned the corner on our regular beat, and we called the ambulance. It looks funny, what the guard said, but not a bank job anyway—just this guy shot. He's assistant manager of the bank, and he was just coming in. You'll get all there is to get from the guard, I guess. The guy who got shot is Lester Mordway, man about fifty, not dead but he didn't look too good. The guard is William Hooker."

The guard, an elderly man, had kept his head; he was retired from the Santa Monica force. "We'd just opened," he told them. "I was surprised Mr. Mordway was late, he was usually here before ten o'clock. I'd just unlocked the front doors—there were only two or three people waiting, we don't as a rule get a lot of people in early, except at the first and last of the month. And the couple of people waiting had just come past me when I saw Mr. Mordway at the door, and I said to him, Good morning, Mr. Mordway, like always, and he nodded to me and just then somebody said his name—I couldn't see who, no, somebody outside the door, just, Mr. Mordway, like that, and he turned to see who it was. Well, I couldn't say about what kind of voice, just a voice, a man's, that's all. And just then this woman asked me some question and I turned to answer her—she wouldn't be anything to do with it, because she's a regular customer, and she was asking about one of our tellers who's been off sick. And just a minute or two later I heard shots out in the street, and I ran out, and there was Mr. Mordway lying there—"

"Where exactly?" said Grace.

He led them out to show them. "Just up there by the alley. Where the side entrance is. He was lying on the sidewalk, but as if he'd been about to go into the alley, all I can say. I rushed up, I saw he was shot, and just before I saw the patrol car and hailed it, he said something. I don't know if I heard it right, or what he meant—he said, 'They said,' and then either 'got' or 'God' or maybe 'bought'—it didn't make much sense."

"Was he fully conscious then?" asked Palliser.

"I wouldn't like to say, sir. He was conscious, but maybe sort of in shock. No, I didn't see anybody running away, but whoever it was—and why anybody'd want to shoot Mr. Mordway God alone knows—whoever it was could've run up the alley there, and got behind the building before I came out."

"What about the shots? Heavy gun?"

"It sounded like a big gun. Of course there's traffic noise, but I didn't stop to wonder if they were shots, like you could confuse a .22 with backfires. I'd say it was a big gun."

That was confirmed when they talked to the doctor at Central Receiving. Nobody else at the bank or around there could tell them anything. The doctor in the emergency ward said that Mordway was in critical condition: bullet wounds in left side, abdomen, and right thigh; he'd lost a lot of blood, he was still unconscious and probably would be for some time, even if he lived at all.

"When you get the slugs out, send them to our lab," said Palliser. The doctor said he knew all about that.

And part of the job, of course, was breaking the bad news. They had the address from the bank, and drove up to Mordway's house on Parnell Avenue in West Hollywood, and told his wife. She was a fluffy blonde in a pink pantsuit, and her tears seemed a little overdone. She only said she couldn't imagine anyone having a reason to shoot Lester before she rushed off for the hospital in a new Impala.

"It looked a little offbeat till just now," said Palliser. "Not that you can type people, but the ones who are so demonstrative, if that's the word, it doesn't usually go very deep with them. The patrolmen said Mordway's about fifty. She's a good deal younger."

"All true," said Grace. "But people—forever all sorts. If he makes it, he can probably give us some idea who shot him."

They went back to the office and gave Wanda their notes to type up. She was silent and grave this morning. Hackett was sitting at his desk drinking black coffee. "It's better than sitting around worrying," he said, "but damned annoying. Business as usual. A couple of new ones—nothing to make much work, I hope—body down on Temple, George went out on it, and an attempted heist at a drugstore."

"At ten A.M.?" said Palliser.

"Time means nothing to the punks," said Hackett. "I heard about this damned ridiculous ransom note. Ten G's!"

"We said it, we said it." Grace came back with a paper cup of coffee. He had sponged his jacket as best he could, but looked ruefully at the stain. "But it is a ransom note, Art. Which makes it definite, a snatch. What did you do to Koutros?"

"Nothing!" said Hackett violently. "I don't like him— he's a loner and just the kind to hold a grudge forever. But he didn't scare, even with George flexing his muscles at him. About those threats he'd made on the lieutenant, just a lot of foolishness that didn't mean anything. And he offered us an alibi for yesterday morning, not asking why. He was at a barbershop at nine-thirty getting his hair cut, and then at Penney's buying shirts. We checked the barber. But that *damned* silly ransom note—"

"He's got to play it straight," said Palliser. "In case. You know that."

"I know it."

"I'm just as glad," said Grace seriously, "I'm not a rich man."

A man came fast and loud into the office, ignoring Lake's exclamation, and looked around angrily. "Bunch of dump cops sitting on your asses—I'm here to say I want some action! What the hell are you doing to find what bastard give my little girl that Goddamned dope? These bastards oughta be hung—if I could get my hands on him —as sure as my name's Jack Hawley I'd tear him apart! My sweet little girl—What the hell are you *doing* about it?"

Palliser got up wearily.

Richness was a relative thing, thought Mendoza as he shut the briefcase on the green paper. The paper was worthless, a bunch of I.O.U.'s, which might shortly become evident to everybody. The only reason the paper had been there handy, in the security vault, was that Mendoza had collected it, part of it, for another cash deal in the silver and gold to go into the safe under the floor of the bedroom at home. The loot the old miser had secretly amassed, turning up to surprise everybody. So lucky they'd been, said Alison. And Luis Rodolfo Vicente Mendoza was no miser; the money didn't mean so much to him, both he and Alison had done without it and could again. But if you had the amassed capital, and any modicum of common sense, you took steps to protect it. Put it in something that would always hold value.

Even the silver and gold were worth nothing against these lives. And he knew coldly what the odds were—pay over ten times this much, no guarantee. The twins, a mysterious part of himself, his hostages to fortune come to him so late, could be twenty-four hours dead by now. But he had to play the hand straight.

The Feds annoyed him, the conscious professionals. They were, he thought, like little boys playing 007. In their unostentatious way they'd set up a command post at the corner of Macy Street, down from the Union Station; they had walkie-talkies and code-signals, the whole damned silly rigmarole.

He took an instant and violent dislike to the professional tail, a cadaverous youngish man named Zachary, with a face like a skull and a pair of completely unemotional, cold slate-gray eyes. These men were supposed to know what they were doing.

Warren was looking at his watch. "Go," he said. He pulled out the walkie-talkie. "W-2 to Zebra. Code M now on way."

It was all ridiculous, as having anything to do with a small pair of human beings who read to him out of McGuffey's Eclectic Reader; with Terry, who was so unhappy over the smallest stain on a dress, with Johnny who still confused O with A. With Alison, who had so belatedly taught him that for every man there is just the one woman.

He walked down to the corner and around it onto Alameda. Not far off was the new jail facility, where he'd been responsible for sending so many miscellaneous offenders against the law. Where, he hoped remotely, this particular offender would end up. Not that that was the important thing. Half a block up he turned into the tiled red-brick foyer of the Union Station. If there was any reality to the ransom note at all, X's eyes—or somebody's—were on him now. He went across from there to the half-open court where the ranks of twenty-four-hour lockers stood. He picked one at random, put in the coin: the key shot into the slot, and he opened the locker and put the briefcase inside. He left the key in the lock, turned and started back up the block.

He didn't know where Zachary was. They had cars spotted around too: Zachary was somewhere with binoculars, to get a clear view of those lockers.

& *will leve note abot kid.*

Mendoza thought, the deliberate illiteracy? The note was over in Questioned Documents; he had wrested it away from the Feds, who had been annoyed. Anything the lab could get, from the pen, the printing, would be got. But, the singular? Why? Not that it mattered right now.

He got back into the unmarked sedan they were using, parked on the street. Warren's silly command post. It was just three o'clock.

"Now we wait," said Warren.

They waited. At intervals one of the walkie-talkies crackled and a voice came over. "Zebra to W-2. Nothing shows yet. Continual observation." Mendoza's head began to ache. He put out a cigarette after three drags on it. He was supposed to be a pro too; he knew how these things went.

At three fifty-nine the walkie-talkie snapped into life. "Zebra to W-2. Subject approaching location. Stand by. . . . Zebra. Subject has picked up package. Cannot tell if anything replaced at location. Repeat, cannot see if anything placed at location. Subject on foot to Alameda. Out." A short pause. Then, unemotionally, "Zebra. S-5, stand by to pick me up corner Alameda and Ducommun. Subject has entered Checker cab at Alameda and Commercial. . . . S-10, come in. Cruise north on Alameda please. . . . Cab is proceeding up Alameda, north. Plate commercial E-247-950, do you want repeat on that?"

It was all very much like little boys playing spy, or cops and robbers. Mendoza realized all of a sudden that he felt very empty; his stomach rumbled embarrassingly.

He said, "The locker. If anything was left—" And he sounded exactly like any muddleheaded citizen, any anxious parent. Warren looked at him kindly.

"Just wait for it."

Valenti's walkie-talkie dispensed a different voice. "S-4 to W-2. The locker is empty. Repeat, nothing in locker." Mendoza heard that with, curiously, no emotion at all. He knew he had expected it. They had all expected it. But they had to play the hand, however bad it was.

By the rules. There used to be rules. He shook his head muzzily. So, nothing: no message. He thought, Koutros?—and I laughed at Danvers. He thought, Berry—and what could anyone say to the poor devil? He thought, that damn-fool story in the *Times*, and anybody—anybody at all, of the wild ones in the city jungle, who might be pleased to get back at a cop, take some loot at the same time—

Deuces wild, he thought. But in that game, the joker was wild too, and could be anywhere in the deck. Anywhere, unless the deck was stacked. And he thought of Hackett saying, Fate.

"Zebra to W-2. Subject has left cab. Is entering apartment house at four-oh-one-three Eagle Avenue. S-5, continue to tail cab. S-11, proceed east to four hundred block Fifth, to rear of apartment building middle of block."

"Let's go," said Warren suddenly, and the silent driver started the engine.

"Talk about amateur efforts," said Valenti disgustedly.

"S-11 to Zebra. Building has no rear exit. Repeat, no rear exit. We are standing by."

Warren barked into the walkie-talkie, "W-2 to Zebra.

Description of subject! . . . What the hell, amateurs—"

The unemotional voice responded at once. "Subject female Caucasian approximately age forty, medium height, one-sixty, blond, wearing blue print dress and white sandals. . . . S-3 reports Checker cab cruising Olive Avenue, no passengers."

"Now what the *hell?*" said Valenti.

"W-2 to Zebra. What is size of building?"

"Zebra. Four units only. Subject is inside, definitely. Do you want S-5 to front?"

"Yes!" said Warren, and snapped the walkie-talkie shut. "A Goddamn stupid bunch of amateurs—Zachary couldn't have missed her. No rear exit! A teaser! This is damn silly."

"What are you going to do?" asked Mendoza. A female, picking up the loot.

"Walk in and grab her. I don't believe this—but it could be the best news we could hear, Mendoza. If it is a couple of amateurs, and all this sure as hell looks like it."

The street was mostly empty: an old narrow street, dusty and lined with shabby, unpainted buildings, mostly old apartments. A few children played on the sidewalk down from here. There were three cars in front of this apartment, men moving quickly into the building, quiet, not attracting attention. Mendoza plodded after Warren, up rickety worn stairs. Then Zachary was there, his voice indifferent as ever. "No trouble, Dave. One apartment empty. Left rear's only one left, the ground floor's clean."

Warren shoved the bell beside that door. There was no name plate. Men waited on both sides of Mendoza. It seemed incredible that it was still daylight, after this long day. A shaft of westering sunlight hit the door from a hall window, and struck full on the woman who opened it cautiously. Her pale blue eyes widened in sudden alarm, understanding, fury; and just as suddenly Mendoza felt himself come alive again, awake and aware, and he shouldered Warren aside savagely.

"¡*Diez millones de demonios negros desde el infierno!*" he said, and out of instinctive knowledge he struck that foolish fat face backhanded, violently, and she fell against the door jamb hard.

"Goddamn cop—" She whimpered. "You Goddamn cops—"

"Here, for God's sake, Mendoza—"

Mendoza flung off Warren's hand. "You're going to ask if I know this female?" he said hardly. "I do. She's one Ruth Ivy, and her husband's a strong-arm thug with a fat package named Walter Ivy, and I'll hear right now just what the hell the pair of you is doing in this business!"

It ended down at headquarters, with Hackett, Higgins and Palliser called in.

They picked up Walter Ivy just as he was taking over the Checker cab to work the night shift. The day shift cabbie had just obliged him, to pick up the missus on an errand. The ten thousand in green paper was stashed under the rear-floor-mat where Walter could retrieve it as soon as he'd taken over the cab.

"What the hell?" he said aggrievedly. "So I heard what the big-man cop said—" He jerked his head at Higgins, at Hackett. "Grillin' me about some heist—I been clean. I heard enough, a snatch on the damn boss's kid. I just had the little idea, if I could work it—Jesus' sake, I don't know nothing about any snatch, I just thought I could grab some easy loot—"

"My sweet Jesus," muttered Hackett. They had a look at the door of that interrogation room: the latch was defective. "Coincidence—for the love of *God!*"

The woman peered up at Mendoza where he stood

chain-smoking, tie loose, collar loose, mouth a grim line. "I didn't want to try any such thing, at first. Somebody's kid maybe kidnapped—even a cop's. But ever'body knows you got a lot o' money. Walter said, easy. No sweat. But honest, we don't know nothing about any kidnapping. What happened to the kid. Walter just—"

"Luis, what the hell can we say? That damn door—"

"*¿Para qué?*" said Mendoza. The little burst of adrenalin had worked its way out of him now. And Warren was efficient. Have a look at Ivy's associates: get a search warrant: it was possible he was doublecrossing somebody. But knowing Walter's record, Mendoza didn't think it was very likely. "I'm going home," he told Hackett.

When he turned the Ferrari up toward the garage, Cedric was sitting there patiently, down by the back wall, keeping vigil.

----------------------- Seven

Both Hackett and Higgins were supposed to be off on Thursday. "There's not one damned thing I can do," said Hackett to Angel, "except help out on the routine. I wish to God we could find that Berry. No, I don't know if I really think he could have—I don't know anything, damn it." Angel looked at him with troubled eyes and said he might as well go in as fidget around home. And she only wished she knew what to say to Alison.

"Damn it," said Higgins to Mary, "there's nothing I can do but sit and worry there instead of here. Well, there's always something to *do*. And, Goddamn it, you know what the answer is—"

"I don't know," said Mary. "And neither do you, George. That awful business yesterday doesn't mean it isn't a real kidnapping."

"I'm going in," said Higgins miserably, reaching for a tie. "They'd let me know if anything turned up, but—"

"I want to call Alison, but there's just nothing to say to her," said Mary. As they went out to the kitchen Steve Dwyer came in with Brucie at his heels.

"Hey, George, it's your day off—you got to go in? Something came up?"

"Something," said Higgins. He wished something would: some answer, however bad, anything so they'd know for certain.

Everybody was there. Mendoza had called in at eight: nothing. And there was always something to do, the inevitable routine, and nothing much more to say.

Pomeroy's witnesses had picked out the mug shot of Theodore Podmore as a possible match for that sketch. They had a couple of addresses listed for Podmore, and ought to go looking for him. Piggott went out on that. There was yesterday's new one, Mordway; Palliser called the hospital and was told that Mordway was still on the critical list, still unconscious. He called Ballistics and got Scarne. The hospital had sent over the slugs out of Mordway, three of them. "So did you make them?" he asked Scarne.

"It's an oldie," said Scarne. "A Browning automatic. If you ever come across it, we can match it up all right, plenty of distinctive marks."

But as to who had shot Mordway, or why, there weren't any obvious leads. They ought to talk to his wife, people at the bank, sniff around for any possible personal motive. And they hadn't done much looking at all on Linda Norcott— "Damnation," said Palliser mildly, remembering that that inquest was called for ten o'clock. He was still sitting there of inertia when Higgins came in, and he asked him about the other new body yesterday.

"I hope Wanda's got the report typed. Nothing for us but paperwork. Another of the damn fools," said Higgins gloomily. "Fellow about twenty-five, hooked on the H since he was fifteen, taking the easy way out. He left a note, and I wish the *Times* would publish things like that, if you ask me. If these idiots realized what they're letting themselves in for—" But he was talking mechanically.

An autopsy report came up just then: the body from that hellhole last Sunday. There wasn't much in it. An O.D., barbs, and the corpse's prints didn't show in L. A.'s records so they'd been sent to Washington. By what showed up at the autopsy, the corpse had been a longtime user.

Linda Norcott—Palliser got out the package of her record and looked through it; there was an address, given the latest time she'd been picked up. "I've got to cover this inquest," he said. "You like to go and ask some questions about Linda?" Higgins said he supposed they ought to, took the address and went out.

They were all conscious of the Fed sitting there in the boss's office, waiting for the phone to ring.

Paperwork, thought Piggott, was the bane of the twentieth century. The paperwork was a far cry from this business of bloody multiple murder, but it was what sent him off on another force's business here, and he didn't think much was going to come of it. He had seen that sketch, and he had seen Podmore's mug shot, and to him they didn't match. The sketch had a wild look about it: Podmore just looked weak.

But, faithful plodder that he was, he tried the first address listed on Podmore's rap-sheet, which was North Hollywood, and interrupted an irascible middle-aged woman at breakfast. She told him that Podmore was her brother's son and she'd made every allowance for that fool of a woman he had married, even let them live here when they were down on their luck after her brother was killed in the accident, but when Theo had taken to forging her checks she'd had enough. She didn't know where they were living now.

Piggott tried the second address, which was in Boyle Heights, and found a sallow, pimply-faced youth who said oh, yeah, Theo used to live there, shared the room with him and another guy, but when he got sick he went home. To his ma. To be took care of.

"Where's home?" asked Piggott.

"Gee, I dunno. Somewhere around here, I guess. His ma works at a Thrifty drugstore, I heard him say."

Going through channels, it took quite a little time to work that lead: the Thrifty chain was a big one with a lot of drugstores scattered through the county. But he ran into an efficient girl in the head personnel office, and at eleven-fifty she found a Mrs. Molly Podmore who was employed part-time at a Thrifty drugstore in Monterey Park: home address on Dover Way.

If he had been convinced he was tracking down one of the multiple murderers, Piggott might have felt more excited; as it was, it was just a tiresome piece of routine, and he was worrying about what the lieutenant was going through. That had been quite a thing, that fake ransom note—Hackett talking about coincidences, the latch on that door going on the fritz just then was funny.

On Dover Way, he found both Mrs. Podmore and Theodore home, in a cheap, brightly modernistic apartment. Podmore looked even less like that sketch now, his nose red and his eyes watery. His mother said he'd had a terrible case of the summer flu, been doctoring for three weeks, and of course he hadn't been doing anything wrong, police always coming after him just because he'd been in a little trouble awhile back. She gave Piggott the doctor's name readily.

So that was that. Piggott came back to the office and asked if there was any news about the twins. There wasn't.

Of course the LAPD wasn't the only force that had received the news about Merced's multiple murder, copies of the sketch, and the ident on Podmore. Piggott sent a telex up to Merced, to clear Podmore out of the business.

"And what the hell," Glasser was saying as he came back into the communal office, "NCIC expects us to do with that one—this pair on the assault over in Utah—I'll be damned if I know. California plates and a bumper sticker, I ask you!"

At ten-thirty William Hooker, the guard at that bank, came in to make a statement as he'd been asked to. Palliser was still at the inquest, and Grace talked to Hooker.

"Well, my God, Mr. Grace, it's just like I told you and the sergeant yesterday, I don't know why anybody'd want to shoot Mr. Mordway. He's—" Hooker hesitated, groping for the right words— "a very nice fellow, you know what I mean, but—well—an ordinary guy. A banker. You know what I mean? Set in his ways, I guess you'd say. Sort of formal. Er—colorless. I mean, he comes to work the same time every day, he's nice and polite to the girls, he's good at his job, I know he's been with the bank for over twenty years. But he's—" Hooker gestured— "just an ordinary, er, banker."

"His wife seems to be a good deal younger," said Grace.

"Yes, I guess so. There was a little talk at the bank, not gossip exactly but people interested. He'd been a widower for at least ten years, his first wife died kind of young, and he just got married again last year. I never met the lady—no, I couldn't say where he met her. But my God, Mr. Grace, you don't think—?"

"We're just looking for any possible personal motive," said Grace mildly.

"But—Mr. Mordway!" said Hooker. "Such an ordinary guy! Not that I've ever had any conversation with him,

Mr. Grace, but he's—he's oldfashioned, some of the tellers call him old Mr. Morality—"

"Is that a fact?" said Grace.

"Because he's always asking them not to wear such short skirts, or pants to work. He can't exactly make them, because the time's past employers could lay down the law about that kind of thing, but he's always—I've heard the girls talking—telling them how if they dress that way they're inviting what he calls unwelcome attention. Mind you, I kind of agree with him—some of those girls come to work in skirts that hardly cover their behinds, I don't think it's decent. But—well, you see what I mean, Mr. Grace."

Grace did. He also thought about Mrs. Lester Mordway in her pink pantsuit and wondered if Mr. Mordway—who sounded like the typical upright moral man to be assistant manager of a branch bank—lectured her on her clothes too. He wondered how those two had got together. There were possibilities to be looked at, at any rate. "Did he have any family by his first wife?"

"I'm afraid I don't know," said Hooker. "Way I say, he's—correct. And I don't have anything to do with the banking. I've worked there as guard nearly five years, but I don't think we ever said more than Good Morning, something about the weather. But he's a nice fellow, Mr. Grace, I don't want to give you the wrong impression. The girls laugh at him sometimes, but everybody likes him. He's always honest and fair, what I hear. And to think of him getting shot like that! Mr. Strange called the hospital first thing, they say he's still on the critical list. I sure hope you can find out who did it."

And this was the kind of rather offbeat case that normally would interest Grace quite a lot; he was interested in how Mordway had come to get shot; but right now they were all a lot more concerned about the lieutenant than any of the routine cases. But however that turned out, they'd be working the routine cases, like it or not. He decided that he'd like to talk to Mrs. Mordway. She'd been upset yesterday, or pretending to be; maybe today she'd sit still long enough to answer questions. He didn't think she was a very shrewd female.

Higgins got nothing at the address for Linda Norcott. It was a single apartment, by courtesy, carved out of three back rooms of what had been a ten-room house, on a shabby old street in an old part of Hollywood. The woman who answered the door said she was *Miss* Early, and yes, it was her house. She was a rather good-looking woman, forty or so, nicely dressed; when Higgins mentioned Linda's name she frowned and then looked pleased.

"Oh, her. I can't say I'm surprised the police are after her. She looked decent enough the day she rented the place, but as soon as she moved in, I found out what sort she was. Drinking parties with the radio on half the night, and then she got behind on the rent. I wasn't about to put up with it, I told her to get out. She was only here a month. And you should have seen the place—I had to give it a good turning out, I don't think she so much as dusted the furniture all that while. What? No, I wouldn't know the names of any of her friends and don't care to, bunch of rackety young people all looked alike to me, men with long hair and some with beards, and girls half dressed. What's she done?" asked Miss Early curiously.

"Got herself murdered," said Higgins.

"Luis," said Alison.

"¿Cómo, amada?"

She was standing with her back to him at the bedroom window. She hadn't got dressed yet, and she'd been unconsciously fiddling with the braided rope sash of the amber nylon robe until it had parted in her hand and come undone; it dangled listlessly. "I never thought it was a kidnapper. All that—about the newspaper story, and those men—it's like something on TV. It'd never happen."

"We can't know that," said Mendoza. He came and put his arms around her.

"I do know it. I feel it. But the very worst of it is— we're not *doing anything*. Just waiting. I know there isn't much we can do, but—"

Mendoza was silent for a moment. He knew what Barth, the other men at Wilcox Street, the Feds, would be doing. After a minute he began to tell her, because Alison wasn't a fool or a coward. They'd be looking up every sex pervert, every known child molester in their books for this area, pulling them in to question: that kind often broke down rather easily.

"They'd have been *found*," said Alison in a muffled voice.

"*Por ningun caso*—it doesn't follow." He didn't add to that; he didn't have to. Even in the sprawling complex of the big city, there were many places a small corpse— two small corpses—could lie hidden. He thought of little Katie May, just last June; he thought of the body up in Elysian Park. "And female intuition isn't infallible, *hermosa*. The odds are still fifty-fifty. The snatcher would let suspense build, so we'll be readier to pay."

"Readier!" said Alison. "It's been forty-eight hours, Luis. Forty-eight hours. They're so little. And all—all their lives—we were such fools—protected and—and cosseted and— They're used to breakfast at seven and lunch at— What's happening to them? And Mairí can pray about it, but—I—can't. I can't. And we're just waiting and not doing anything!"

"Easy, *cara*." Over her head he could see, out there in

the yard, part of the slide and the sandbox. There was a cat sitting on the bottom step of the slide, he couldn't see which one. Then Cedric barked, and he heard the old car come up the drive. "That's Mairí home. Do you feel like any breakfast now?"

"No. I'm trying to be good, Luis, I know it's no use going to pieces and acting like a fool, but—they're all we have—and didn't I say it, didn't I know it, we've been too lucky—had too much."

"Now don't be superstitious."

Mrs. MacTaggart's voice raised out in the hall, more emphatically Scottish than usual. Mendoza kissed Alison and turned to the door.

"And I'll thank ye," she was saying dangerously to Valenti, "to stop your fuilish chasin' of a respectable body into church! If ye think I'm such a gey idiot as not to see yer friends taggin' along behind me from the corner up there, juist why should ye think I'm a bluidy criminal conspirin' to kidnap my own darling lambs? And they had the impudence to follow me into church! Into the church, mind— D' ye think Father Dunphy's a kidnapper too?" She was outraged; she faced Valenti with hands on hips, her eyes shooting sparks.

"For God's sake, lady, I just take orders," said Valenti. "It wasn't me."

"Are you telling me—" began Mendoza, but Alison's voice cut across his.

"You damned suspicious fools!" She had heard, and stood at the door clutching the robe about her tightly. The temper that frequently goes with red hair flared in her eyes and shaking voice. "You— ¡Bastardos! ¡Pedazo del alcornoque! ¿No le da verguenza?— ¡Estúpido condenable—loco imbécil!" She let go of the robe and came to put her arms around Mairí. "You can get out of this house—if you haven't anything better to do than— ¡*Por mi vida*! Luis—"

"¡*Despacio*!" said Mendoza.

"Look, I didn't give the orders," said Valenti. "We like to be thorough."

"Thorough!" said Mendoza angrily. "I can't back up my wife on ordering you Feds out, Valenti, but by God I'd like to! I thought Warren had better sense—he's not dealing with the average citizen here, and if he thinks I don't know my own household—"

"Mairí's family!" said Alison furiously. "You damned stupid *necios*—"

"Hey, hey!" said Valenti. "Calm down. I'm sorry, it wasn't me."

"All right— ¡*Bastante*!" said Mendoza. "Go and sit on that damned phone—it'll never ring until Judgment Day." He swung on Alison and Mairí. "Shameless hussy, go and get dressed. I want you to try to eat something—¿*por favor*? Mairí, you calm down and see if you can get some breakfast into her." He marched back to the bedroom and came out with his hat.

"Where are you off to?" asked Valenti apprehensively.

"Out!" said Mendoza.

There had been something in his mind, and he had only pinned it down in the last hour. Something Art had said about coincidence. The lady author saying, never in fiction—unfair. Unfair! Mendoza smiled tightly to himself, thinking of real life as seen by cops, who saw more of it than most people. How many times did coincidence, which might be another name for Fate, take a hand? How many times did the unexpected witness turn up: the random choice of a street to walk down, a turning to make, a window to look out of, change the course of lives? And the joker, wild, could be anywhere in the deck.

He drove the Ferrari rather slowly down to Hollywood Boulevard, stashed it in a lot, and got most of the cash on him changed into coin at the bank on the corner. He shut himself into a public phone booth outside the bank, and called his office first in case anything had happened since he had left the house. Nothing had; he talked to Hackett and let off a little steam about the Feds. Remotely, as he put up the phone, he thought about the cases they'd had on hand last Tuesday morning, and wondered if they were getting cleared up, and what new ones had gone down.

He had looked for a phone booth which boasted all five phone directories. He contemplated them now, stacked up, and lit a cigarette, shoved the homburg back. It was a little joke down at headquarters, Mendoza and his crystal ball; and it didn't operate automatically. Right now he didn't need a crystal ball so much as a lot of imagination.

If you lived somewhere in upper Hollywood and wanted to buy a TV, where would you go? It was like the old question, why is a mouse when it swims? Moreover, if you were in business selling TV's, how would you deliver them?

He smoked slowly, staring at the phone directories. He thought, discount houses. Small places. Secondhand stores (a dismal thought). Classified ads (even more dismal). He fished out change, opened the Hollywood-West L.A. book to the yellow pages, and started dialing. It was nine-fifteen.

There was a drugstore half a block up. At ten-thirty he went up there for a cup of coffee, came back and went on dialing. He was ruthlessly marking the yellow pages as he crossed out numbers. When he came to the end of the list he'd checked with X's in the Hollywood book he started on the downtown directory. That lasted him up to twelve-fifteen. He called his office again: nothing; and went on to the Glendale-Burbank book.

At one forty-five he ran out of change and went to the bank for more. He started on the West-Valley-Van Nuys book.

At two-fifteen he hit the jackpot. "Yeah?" said a surprised voice. "Oh, yeah. We do. Just lately. Who is this? Why you askin'?"

"Police business," said Mendoza. "Can you give me an address?"

"*Police*—well, I'll be damned!" said the voice. "If that isn't the craziest—look, they're both here now. Puttin' on a load. I don't know them too good but they seem like all-right guys, they wouldn't be mixed up in police business, for God's sake."

"I just want to talk to them." Mendoza stepped on his latest cigarette. Jackpot—and what did it mean? But if there was any dominating single force in Luis Mendoza, it was his cold and dispassionate regard for truth, for facts. Whatever truth was, whatever the hard facts were in any given case, it was better to bring them out in the open and look at them. And there, he knew Alison would agree.

There was a different voice on the phone. "*Police?* Jim said you were asking— Well, for God's sake, what's it all about?"

"I'm afraid you may be taking the rest of the day off," said Mendoza. "Stay where you are—I'll be out to talk to you."

The address was on the outskirts of Van Nuys. It was three-twenty when he called Warren; he had used the siren on the freeway. He used it on the way back, and it was four o'clock when he pulled the Ferrari up the drive. Warren was in front talking to Valenti. Mendoza and his passenger got out.

"If you're passionately concerned to have Mrs. Mac-Taggart identify the truck, we can bring it up," he told Warren. "This is Mr. Ben Windrow."

"I ain't sure what this is all about," said Mr. Windrow. "But, oh, gee, that's some car! I never rid behind a sireen before. That's sure some car!" He was young, wiry, frank-looking, with brownish-blond hair straggling below his ears. "Yeah, I guess this is the place. I guess I was off base, but you got to remember I ain't familiar with this place yet, we only been here a couple months."

Mendoza went into the house and brought Mairí out. "Well, for guidness' sake!" she said, staring. "Yon's him— the one I told you about. With the truck and the TV set. Don't tell me—och, ye aren't tellin' me—"

"Nothing, Mairí. A mare's nest," said Mendoza. "So what about it, Windrow? Tell the gentlemen."

"Well, gee, lady, I was off base," said Windrow. "I'm sorry. Gary and me, Gary's my brother, we just started up a little business here—deliveries, see, we got our own truck. We pick up business wherever we can, places can't afford keep their own truck, see. We been doin' some for this discount place out in Van Nuys. Well, see, Gary's some better 'n me at readin' maps and like that, only last Tuesday he was off sick. He had a terrible case o' the trots, see, runnin' to the bathroom every five minutes, so naturally he couldn't go with me. And I had this TV to deliver—" He was looking at their expressions with growing bewilderment. "I sure thought this was the right place—I'm sorry if I give you a bad time, ma'am—but I figured out later it was a house on Rio Grande Street over in Burbank. But what the hell's so important about it?"

"How did you find him?" asked Warren.

"Not with my crystal ball," said Mendoza.

And there was something rather important about it, which he didn't have to explain to Mairí; he saw the little consternation in her eyes. He went in to tell Alison where he'd been all day. He'd let the Feds ferry Windrow back to his truck.

Henry Glasser, that afternoon, had gone out to do the little legwork they would do on the Hawley girl. There was too much dope, of all varieties, and too many suppliers around, to waste time trying to pin down one more; and in a lot of cases the kids passed it around hand to hand, didn't know where it came from themselves.

He talked to four girls who'd known Angie Hawley at school. Three of them didn't tell him anything, wary. The fourth, Michelle Rambo, talked up to a point. She didn't take any stuff herself, she said, except a little grass sometimes, and what was that, nothing, it'd be legal pretty soon. Glasser looked at her sadly. It was peoples' own business, she said, what did it matter? Just like taking a drink, or not so bad, and all the do-good people thought it was so terrible, they took drinks all right. Sure, there was stuff around school; she guessed Angie'd been taking some a couple of years, the kids she went with. It was her business. No, of course she didn't know where it came from.

"You do know she's dead of an overdose?" asked Glasser.

The girl's pert young face suddenly drew a little taut. "Well, it's not such a great world to be alive in, is it? What the hell, pig—you want to know any names, ask somebody else."

Glasser came back to the office at five o'clock and found the rest of them talking about Mendoza's jackpot. He dropped his notebook on Wanda's desk, asked for chapter and verse. "Well, that sort of weights the scale, doesn't it? When we heard about that truck, and the argument about the TV, right about the time the kids went, it looked like a set up diversion to get the nurse away from the kitchen, where she could see the back yard. Now it turns out to be a big fat damned coincidence. So I say again, I'm sorry, but I think it was the pervert."

"Henry, it's more than two days," said Wanda. "They'd have been found. And the perverts don't always kill them—in fact, that's the exception. I know it's horrible to think about, but—"

"It ain't necessarily so?" said Glasser sleepily. "Even roundabout here, places they could be. And there've been a lot of cases—" He was silent, and then went on, "We don't like to talk horrors, lady, but you've got to face the facts. This makes it look the hell of a lot less likely it was a snatch. That puts it right back to the nut. And most people, nuts or not, have access to a car. That is the hell of it. The *hell* of it. Those two poor kids—"

Hackett was looking sick. Higgins just looked grim. Grace said, eyes shut, "That would always be the worst of it, not knowing. That baby that got snatched from a parking lot, they never did find him. All those co-eds raped and murdered back east, when they caught up to X he tried to show where he'd buried two of them but they couldn't locate the bodies. Wild country, but even so— How many cases in *True Detective*, somebody disappears, somebody any age and place, and—if the luck runs that way—a couple of years later somebody else stumbles on a skeleton. Or not. That waitress over in Vegas, they didn't find her for three years."

"Stop it!" said Wanda. "I know that kind of thing happens, Jase. But we've got to hope—we've got to do a little praying on it. And if you talk about coincidence, I think it'd be another pretty farfetched one, that just that five minutes the nurse didn't have them in sight, this nut

134

all fortuitously turned up and spirited them away without a sound!"

"The nuts are all around," said Glasser. "Like the coincidences. I'll grant you it does seem funny they didn't yell."

Hackett moved and the chair creaked under his bulk. "Alison was saying something to Angel," he said heavily. "Cops' kids—supposed to be all carefully warned. But they're not four, they've always been—looked after. Johnny'd go to anybody offered him a ride in a car—and Terry's used to tagging after Johnny."

Wanda burst into tears. "You can talk about facing facts all you want—I think you're horrible, talking as if it's all over—"

"Facts," said Glasser sadly, but he followed her out. Higgins got up and said he was going home, to be called if anything broke. Sergeant Lake had already gone, and there was a different Fed sitting in Mendoza's office. Piggott stood up and frowned down at the floor.

"A lot of people," he said, "come to a lot of far-out conclusions trying to make sense out of prophecy in the Bible. Daniel, and Revelations. I don't altogether go along with what our minister says about it. There've been too many people thought they had it figured out, and then found out they were wrong. Some of 'em thought the world would come to an end in 1843, but here we are still perking along."

"After a fashion," said Grace.

"But one thing I will say. Satan going up and down and far and wide," said Piggott. "It does say he'll have power for a little time." He shook his head and went out quietly.

"Art," said Palliser abruptly. He had sat there smoking, silent, for the last ten minutes.

"Um?"

"You like to do a little overtime tonight? Speaking of ministers, that Hatch. There doesn't seem to be anything to get hold of on it. I went back over it today—if it's going into Pending, we ought to work it a little first. Nobody seems to have known much about him—a solitary, wrapped up in his church work, and nothing showed up, any arguments with people, or women or money troubles—everybody looked up to him."

"So?"

"Well I don't know if I had a little hunch on it. What was he doing down there on Olympic? The car was in good condition, he hadn't got stalled. I went and looked at that block, and it's all shops that would be closed by six. The only place open would be that tavern. And it just occurred to me—it's really reaching—but, that combo playing there. Hatch was doing some counseling work with drug addicts. He was concerned. Musicians—to use the word loosely—sometimes are addicts. And we don't know he wasn't counseling some of them privately. I'd just like to see that combo. It's the only nebulous connection I can come up with."

"Wild," said Hackett. "But it's O.K. with me. I'd rather go out on a wild-goose chase than sit at home stewing and fussing. I'll meet you here at eight-thirty, O.K.?—unless something breaks."

Warren called Mendoza at the new number at eight-thirty. "Ivy looks clean of any possible connection. He's been on P.A. for a year, just off, working that regular job with the cab company, and he's never been a bigtimer, no association with anything like that."

Mendoza laughed. "Teach your grandmother! I could have told you that. It was just a damned coincidence he overheard the boys and thought he'd get in on the act. Is that all you've got to say?"

"Windrow checks out clean too."

"*Gracias*—I thought he would." Mendoza put the phone down and discovered that Alison had left the bedroom: small sounds of distress came down the hall and he trailed them to the nursery. The erstwhile nursery.

Mairi's stern Scottish control had given away. She was rocking back and forth, weeping silently, a worn stuffed dog of Terry's clutched between her hands. "Where are they, *achara*? My dear wee lambs—you sayin' like a grandmother, och, I heard you, and it's juist like so I feel—never any o' my own—where are they this nicht?"

"Mairí, darling—we've just got to hope—" Alison's voice was choked.

Mendoza left her to deal with it. When she came back to the bedroom he was standing at the window, pajama-clad, smoking. The cats were coiled at the foot of the bed. He said without turning, "I could recommend a small drink."

"*Sí, amado, gracias.*" She sat down on the bed and El Señor woke up and hissed at her. A moment later, hearing the bottle of rye taken down from the cupboard, he fled to beg his share.

"Señor *Ridículo*," said Mendoza, and poured him an ounce.

Cedric was out in the yard, anxious by the back wall.

Alison took a sip of the rye and said, "Luis. I can add two and two. That man Windrow—it makes a little difference. If he was—a diversion, for Mairí, it must have been a planned thing. But I never believed that. And now, it looks—more likely—like the other thing. Doesn't it?"

"*Querida*, we take it as it comes. *Quien supo olvidar no supo amar.*"

"Luis," she said abstractedly. "Luis—whether we find them or not—whether we get them back or not—I think we'd better have another one right away. *¿Cómo no, marido?*"

"We'll think about it," said Mendoza gently.

It was the only thing alive in the dark block, the pink neon, *Ted's Place*. "You see what I mean," said Palliser. "And it was later than this. The autopsy said between nine and twelve."

"I still say it's reaching," said Hackett.

They went into the tavern. It was a typical neighborhood place, attracting the young married people, young working people. It didn't have a hard liquor license, wine and beer only. The combo had just come in and were setting instruments up on the little raised platform next to the bar. The genial fat barkeep-owner was dispensing drinks and conversation to an obviously regular clientele. There'd be innocent dancing and merriment, in a quiet way, and the place closed down at midnight; it wasn't café society.

Palliser threaded his way among tables up to the platform. He had the badge out, unobtrusively. "Like to ask you a few questions," he said.

The piano player, a fat young man in loud sports clothes, looked at them cynically and said, "For God's sake. We had cops in last, when was it, Sunday night— something about a body out in the street. We didn't know nottin' about, *paisano*. Big city—bodies all around these days, no?"

The sax player was already sitting down, fingering his horn; he scowled at them. The drummer was setting up all his traps, snare, bass with the pedal, a trio of cymbals. He was a thin dark young fellow with a wisp of moustache.

"You told Detective Conway," said Palliser, "that you'd stepped out in front for a minute when you took a break at—what time?—about ten that night."

The drummer glanced sideways at him. "That's right."

"And there wasn't any car in the street then?"

"No." He dropped a cymbal and the crash was loud. He retrieved it with shaking hands. "No."

"What's your name?" asked Palliser. Mendoza had once told him never to be afraid to play his hunches, but this hadn't been a hunch, only a very far-out idea.

"Uh—Archie Fellows. I don't know anything about it."

"A minister by the name of Hatch?" said Hackett suddenly, looming up beside Palliser. "Who was interested in drug addicts?"

Fellows uttered an inarticulate cry and fled, taking everybody by surprise, up the little tavern toward the front door. Hackett and Palliser plunged after him, and caught up in the street outside. "I never meant to do such a thing!" cried Fellows in agony. "I never meant it!"

"You knew Hatch from the clinic?" said Palliser.

"Don't you dare say I ever took any dope in my life!" said Fellows furiously. "It was my brother went to that place—my God, I've been scared to death, I never meant—but that Goddamned *minister!* Barry liked him, and I didn't know what to do—I've got to say he helped Barry, and if I told about it, maybe Barry'd backslide again—I didn't know what the hell to do! But when that Goddamned minister came at me—"

"What do you mean?"

"Well, my God, he was a fag—a homo—for God's sake, I never meant to kill him, but I had to protect myself!" Fellows subsided, panting a little.

"You had a far-out idea," said Hackett to Palliser. "Just not far enough."

------------------------ Eight

"Get away!" said Conway, his cynical gray eyes amused. "The minister?"

Fellows had come along docilely and was only too ready to talk. He said despondently, slumped in a chair beside Hackett's desk, "I guess this might set Barry back a lot worse. But I didn't know what to do. First I thought nobody'd believe me—that old bastard covered his tracks, I bet, all so holy and righteous! But some reason, he took a notion to me. It was damn *embarrassing*. Damn it, I'm a married man! And Barry—"

"So what happened on Sunday night?" asked Hackett.

Fellows looked morosely at his hands—square, spatulate, strong, musician's hands. "Well, he knew I was playing there—three nights a week we make Ted's, and the Del Rio Friday and Saturday. He used to pretend he wanted to talk to me about Barry, see? And he came that night—to Ted's—I saw him look in the door about ten to ten, wanting me to come out. And I thought, God's sake, what am I gonna do about him? I just made up my mind, I'll go out and talk up to him straight, tell him to—to buzz off, he can take his dirty fag's trick someplace else. So at the break I went out, I got in his car and I started to do that, I cussed him out—Jesus, a minister, and everybody thinking—! But it seemed like he wasn't listening, and then he got his hands on me—Jesus, I know this sounds kind of silly but I panicked, I wasn't about to let him—"

"Your knife, Mr. Fellows?" asked Palliser.

"Yeah, yeah. I told you, five nights a week we're playing jobs—it's how I earn a living—and I'm coming home after midnight, not such a hot neighborhood. I never used it before." Fellows mopped his brow. "My God, I didn't know he was dead until these cops come in! I like to passed out! I thought I just jabbed him a few times, make him let me go—my God! And now you know about it—my God, will they say I murdered him? Me? I never meant to kill the old son of a bitch—"

"Well, we can't promise you how the courts will look at it," said Palliser, "but in the circumstances it's very possible it'll be called manslaughter and you'll get off light, Mr. Fellows. But right now, I'm afraid you're under arrest."

"Yeah, I figured," said Fellows mournfully. "Can I call my wife?"

They would let Wanda get out the report in the morning. Hackett took him over to the jail and booked him in.

The night watch had heard about Mendoza's jackpot, and looked soberly at the day men, knowing what it probably meant.

Just after Hackett and Palliser left, they had a call from Traffic. There had been that A.P.B. out on Joel Fliegel's car, and a black-and-white had just come across it parked at the curb on Grand. Conway went down to look at it. The hood was up, and the battery unhooked.

"Educated guess," said one of the patrolmen, focusing his flashlight, "it died on him and he'll be back with a new battery."

"Not tonight," said Conway. The car was still faintly warm; it hadn't been here long. It might be just worthwhile, he thought, to ask Traffic to stake out the car as soon as it was light, and repair shops open. Or it could be that Fliegel had abandoned it. But he seemed to remember that Fliegel was said to be an expert mechanic: it could be that he'd turn up with a new battery. That garage where he'd once worked, they knew now, hadn't seen him lately, but there were a lot of garages.

"Who is he? We just got the all-points on the car."

"Hooked up to a bank job in Sacramento," said Conway.

Piggott had said hardly a word over dinner, not even expanding on the office view of the delivery man the lieutenant had found, and Prudence was exasperated. Preserving Christian patience, she watched him standing in front of the fish tank staring into space until she couldn't stand it, and asked him what was the matter.

Piggott was not a swearing man, but his pauses could be eloquent. After a moment he said, "There's been something right on the tip of my mind all day, Prue, and I just can't pin it down. But it's about that Berry—Arnold Berry. You know, I went out on that arson case with Henry. The Fire Department called us in because of the people getting killed in the fire, on our beat. And I talked to this Berry then. I don't know what the—what it is, but it's something about—that I just can't bring to the surface."

"If it's important it'll come to you," said Prudence. "Just make a little prayer about it and forget it—it'll come."

"I hope so," said Piggott. And whether it was the

prayer or his subconscious mind, he woke up at four A.M., sat straight up in bed, and said, "My God!"

Prudence stirred and mumbled.

"That was it! And it could be—" Piggott looked at the bedside clock, compressed his lips, and thought a minute. The night watch was gone. But he figured this could be important enough to wake people up and tell them. He went out to the phone in the hall and dialed Hackett's house in Highland Park. Years of discipline change natural habits; Hackett answered on the fourth ring, sounding reasonably alert.

"—And all of a sudden it came to me, in a dream or something. Listen, Art. When I was talking to Berry that time—it was just after the fire, you remember, that is a couple of days after—he was still in a little state of shock. Talking about his wife and the two daughters—but one thing he said was about this mountain cabin they had up by Crystal Lake, how they all liked to go there. It just occurred to me, if he's still got it—and that was only about two months ago—it might be just the place he'd go to brood."

"By God," said Hackett, fully awake, "and just the place he might think of—Thanks, Matt. I think we move on this. It could also be the reason that A.P.B. hasn't turned up a smell of him. I'm going to call Luis."

Mendoza had made Alison take a sleeping tablet, but he hadn't been to sleep at all. He grabbed for the new phone beside the bed, got it on the first ring, and she didn't stir. Listening to Hackett, he felt a little cold excitement rise in his mind. Maybe because he'd been too close to it, not since he'd heard Alison's voice last Tuesday morning had he had any feeling, any small intuition, damn the hunch, about this; now he did, very faintly. Berry could be the answer. This could be the answer—what kind, he wasn't ready to contemplate.

"The Rangers," he said. "It'll be light in an hour. Call the Rangers in on it, find out if he's there—they can locate the cabin. But with extreme caution, Art. Emphasis added—¡no tocar!"

"Why?"

"Berry isn't a pro thug or a criminal of any kind. He's an ordinarily decent man who's had the hell of a shock, and maybe he's temporarily a little crazy. He's not a pervert or a killer, whatever he said the other day. There's a chance, if he's got them, he's still deciding what to do."

"And maybe he's already done it," said Hackett. "Being temporarily crazy."

"I said a chance, damn it! I'll meet you at the office." Mendoza flung on some clothes, left a hasty note for Alison, and started out. The Fed was asleep out in the hall; there was a light under Mairí's door but she didn't stir. He backed the Ferrari out to the turn of the circular drive and made tracks; at that hour there wasn't any traffic.

When he got down to Parker Center there was just a faint gray light in the sky. Up in the office, Hackett was looking slightly rumpled from hasty dressing; and Higgins came in a minute behind Mendoza. "I've already contacted the Ranger Station up there," said Hackett; he was sitting on the switchboard. Crystal Lake was in the huge wilderness of the Angeles National Forest. "They're checking."

It was nearly light when the Ranger Station called back, in the person of Ranger Farwell. "We've located Berry's cabin, Sergeant. It's northeast of the lake, pretty lonely spot, not much else around. I'm on my way out there now, talking from the car. We'll let you know if he's there."

"Be careful—don't spook him if he is."

"Will do." Five minutes later Farwell said, "His car's there, in the carport. I'm on a ridge above, with glasses.

144

It's his car all right, the plate-number you gave us. What do you want?"

Mendoza's long-fingered hand came down on Hackett's shoulder; the call was on the amplifier. "If there's anything to this, I want to handle it. It just could be—Berry knows me—he'd listen to me and nobody else. ¿Todo o nada, cómo no? We can be up there in an hour."

"I always said it could go back to Berry," said Higgins. "You're not going without me."

Mendoza took the phone. "Leave him alone," he said. "We're coming up. Plan some strategy when we get there. Meanwhile, keep an eye on him. If he moves you can stop him. Otherwise, wait for us. At the Ranger Station."

"Will do," said Farwell laconically.

They commandeered a squad car from Traffic and rode the siren all the way, through Glendale, Pasadena, Monrovia, up the San Gabriel Canyon Road, to the Ranger Station near the bottom of the road to Mount Wilson. It was seven-thirty A.M. when they got there.

Hackett had left a note for the day men. "Berry," said Palliser thoughtfully. "It could be why he hasn't been picked up."

"I could have kicked myself for not thinking of it before," said Piggott. "A little thing, it went right out of my mind." This was supposed to be his day off.

"Well, if Berry is the answer, he's not a nut or a thug," said Glasser. "Which is the reason I don't think he is the answer." Wanda, excited, told him he was a pessimist.

"When will we know anything?"

"God knows—Art'll call in," said Palliser. "Hold some good thoughts on it."

And meanwhile, there were cases to be worked on. The inquest on Beatrice Anderson was scheduled for this morning; someone would have to cover that. Just before the night watch went off last night there'd been an attempted heist, at a twenty-four-hour café that catered mostly to truckers, down by the Stack. Galeano had left a note about it. Reading it, Glasser said that it rang a faint bell.

"The one heister the witnesses said was short and thin. Here he is again, I think, but he didn't get anything." Glasser went down there to get a fuller description if possible, and found the owner, Pat Halloran, just leaving, the day counterman taking over.

"I had to take night shift since Eddy's off sick," he told Glasser. "Just as well last night maybe, Eddy's no hand with a gun. When this joker came in, it was a slack time, see, just before midnight, no customers in—I guess he waited for that—and he shows me the gun. I think it coulda been a .32, yeah, a revolver. And two can play that game, mister, I reached under the counter and showed him mine. Hah!" said Halloran explosively. "Most of these punks don't hardly know how to hold a gun—think the look of it makes 'em the big man. I said, I give you one warning, punk, out, I says, and he didn't go right off so I fired a shot at him."

"Get him?"

"Well, he yelled, so I guess I did, but not bad because he made tracks outta here like the devil was after him. What? Yeah, he wasn't very big, about five-five, and thin—nope, no mask—I'd put him about twenty-five, kind of medium coloring."

"That's very good," said Glasser. "We think he's the same boy who pulled a couple of others around here."

"Well, he got scared last night," said Halloran. "Good luck on finding him."

Back at the office, Palliser and Grace kicked around the Berry thing for a few minutes, and Palliser called the hospital. Mordway was still unconscious but holding his own, slightly improved.

"That is a funny little thing," said Grace. Palliser agreed.

"We can't disturb the citizens until a decent hour." It was eight-forty. "I wonder if they're finding anything up there. On the one hand, it's far out, but on the other—"

"People." Grace had been cynically amused about the answer on Hatch. When you thought about it, maybe a comment on this period of history: Matt would say so. "If we stop for another cup of coffee, we ought to find Mrs. Mordway up by nine."

"Take no bets. I wonder what her first name is."

They pulled up in front of the Mordway house on Parnell Avenue at nine-five. At any other time they'd have been more interested in this funny business, but right now half their minds were up there with Mendoza, wondering what was turning up.

It was a nice house, nothing grand but substantial, tan stucco and permanent awnings beyond a green lawn. They had to wait at the door quite a while, and when she opened it she was wearing a pink nylon robe trimmed with fake feathers, and gold mules.

"Well, what on earth do you want?" she asked crossly. "Come here at the crack of dawn."

"It's about your husband, Mrs. Mordway—"

"Oh—ho isn't—he isn't dead?" A curious unreadable look came into her large blue eyes.

"No, no," said Grace. "We've talked to the hospital and he seems to be a little bit better. But we'd still like to get some idea of how he happened to get shot."

"Oh. Yes. It really is the most terrible thing—I just don't understand it. You'd better come in, I suppose." They went into a living room which had a curiously wrong look, and at a second glance Palliser deduced that it had once been a solidly-furnished rather oldfashioned room: there were several pieces of old oak and walnut, respectable Victorian (Mordway digging in his heels to keep those?). Superimposed on it now was a good deal of violently modern furniture, queer-shaped plastic chairs you would need a shoehorn to get out of.

"I just can't understand it," and she shed a few tears prettily into her handkerchief. "Lester getting shot! I thought it might be a bank robbery when they called, but it wasn't, was it?"

"No, ma'am. Had your husband had any trouble with anyone lately? Arguments?"

"*Lester?* Goodness, no. Lester never quarrels with anybody—not even when he thinks I've been a little bit extravagant." She gave them an arch smile. "Well, of course I must say he didn't like it when Arthur said such things about me, but for heaven's sake, Arthur wouldn't shoot him! I just can't make it out—but I'm so terribly, terribly relieved my dear boy's better."

"Arthur?" said Palliser.

"Oh, Arthur's his son. By his first marriage. Children always resent people getting married again, I suppose it's natural," she said vaguely.

"Does he live here? I mean, in this area?"

"Yes, why? Oh, I suppose you want to see him too—I don't know why. He wouldn't know anything. I warn you, my dear policemen, he'll probably say some awful things about me," she told them brightly, smoothing her blond curls, "but it's just talk. Lester said so. Well, of course he knows about it, I hope I know my duty, I called to tell him, Lester's his father after all. But I don't know what you think either of us'd know about it. It happened at the bank."

In the Rambler, Grace said, "I think we talk to Arthur."

"So do I."

Arthur Mordway, who worked at a brokerage firm but was too upset about his father to be at work, was a straightforward young man with a good jaw. He had a house in West Hollywood and a pretty, darkhaired wife. "Dad getting shot!" he said. "I didn't believe it at first, and then—but it wasn't that. I'm as much at sea about it, maybe, as you are." He eyed them shrewdly. But when Palliser asked a cautious question about Mrs. Mordway, he went up like a rocket. "Oh, my God, that woman! Thalia—I ask you, what kind of made-up name—I thought Dad had gone crazy, but in a way I can understand why it happened. He had my mother practically bedridden for seventeen years, till she died, and I guess he was all ready to kick over the traces—man that age. Of course the woman's only interested in his money, a comfortable living, she butters him up— For God's sake, you don't think *she* had anything to do with it?" He looked astonished, and then speculative.

"We're just looking for any possible motive for anyone to want him dead," said Grace.

Arthur Mordway rubbed his jaw. "When you put it that way, by God, I've got an idea she might prefer his insurance and annuity and the house to herself."

"Oh, Arthur," said his wife. "That's slander. She's a cheap little gold-digger, but I wouldn't believe—"

"There's that brother of hers," said Mordway. "At least she says he's her brother. Name of Edward Whiting. I've only met him once but I wouldn't put anything past him."

"Oh, Arthur—"

"You don't know where he lives, his job?"

"He's supposed to be a salesman, I don't know where. She'll have his address. My God—Dad!—if it was— But thank God, the doctor says he's got a good chance to make it now."

"Yes, we're glad to hear that. . . . Round and round

the mulberry bush," said Grace in the car. "And this could
be a rather crude thing after all. Find Whiting. But it's
not as urgent as what might have been happening up in
the mountains. Let's go back to base and see if there's
any news."

There was some news.

"Now let's play this easy," said Mendoza. "Let's not
spook him. You're sure he's there?"

"Yep," said Farwell. He and another Ranger, Stass,
had driven Mendoza, Hackett and Higgins to this vantage
point on a little ridge above a hollow in the hills. It was
wild country up here, not covered with dense forest as
parts of the park were, but heavily wooded with smaller
trees, birch and young firs, and thick underbrush. Parts
of the park, farther up in the mountains, held the fash-
ionable summer resorts crowded now—Big Bear, Arrow-
head, the Swiss Colony—but around here were scattered,
few and far between, the humbler summer cabins. "Seen
him with the glasses, moving around inside. If it is Berry."

"*Bueno.* Anybody else?"

"Nope. What do you want to do?"

"Let's move in closer," said Mendoza. "If one of you
can get him to let you in, all nice and easy, and shut the
door, we'll move in behind you. I don't want to—set him
off in any way."

"What's he done?"

"We don't know, but it's possible he's kidnapped my
—children. He thought he had a grudge on me—illogical,
but that's nothing new. But if he's temporarily a little
crazy, he's basically a decent man, and I can't believe—"
Mendoza stopped. He didn't want to believe. But it was
three days now—seventy-two hours.

"God," said Farwell in comment. "Come on. There's
an old road goes to that cabin, not so hot for your springs.

150-

We can stay around the bend down there. Give it a try."

Mendoza heard Hackett breathing quickly beside him. It had been a little pull up this hill and as usual Hackett was carrying a few pounds too much. The cabin down there, with its rudely-built carport at one side, Berry's old car in it, was a modest place. About four rooms, a porch on the front, two windows facing this way. It was built of plain clapboard once painted green, now faded to no color. Right now there was no sign of movement from within.

They backed down off the ridge and the three LAPD men piled into the back of the Ranger's four-wheel-drive. They took the opposite direction from the cabin, but presently turned right onto a rough track that led, curving, around the base of the hill.

"This is as close as we'll get," said Farwell. "The cabin's fifty yards up around that bend."

"All right," said Mendoza. "Let's find some cover up there, and you or Stass go and give him some tale."

With no wasted words they moved up the trail. There was a stand of young pines, fairly thick, just at the bend, and while Farwell went on at an easy stride up the track, the rest of them deployed behind the trees. They had a fair view of part of the cabin front.

Farwell's boots rang on the little porch and he called out in a friendly tone, "Anybody here? Chief Runger, just a little fire inspection tour. Anybody in?"

He called twice more before the cabin door opened slowly. "Mr. Berry?" said Farwell.

"What the hell do you want?" In the clear summer air, at this altitude, his voice came faintly to them.

"Just a little talk with you, Mr. Berry," said Farwell, and put a hand on his arm. "If you'll let me come in a minute, sir—"

"Go to hell!" said Berry, and shook him off with unexpected violence, stepped back and slammed the door.

"That's blown it!" said Hackett, savage; all four of them ran for the open space where the cabin stood, and Mendoza raised his voice almost desperately.

"Berry! This is Mendoza! Listen, Berry, I just want to talk to you—if you've got them there, if they're not hurt, nothing's going to happen to you— Please listen to to me, Berry! If you've—"

A shot crashed through one of the front windows and Farwell yelled and clapped a hand to his leg. They pulled him away from the porch to a clump of underbrush ten yards off. Hackett and Higgins had their guns out. Farwell wasn't hurt badly: a flesh-wound in the calf. "For God's sake, don't fire!" said Mendoza. "Berry!"

Five more shots came blind through the window, and then there was silence. "I wonder how much ammo he's got in there," said Higgins.

But a moment after that, Berry burst out a door at the rear of the cabin and took off down the slope behind, running awkwardly, stiff-legged—a sedentary man, the polite clerk in men's furnishings—running in great leaps, helped by his downward course.

Stass took the lead at once; the others were city men, unused to these hills and hollows covered with dry grass, sage, wild anonymous growth, with sudden rocky screes and unexpected boulders.

As he ran, blind and careless, Berry let fall the gun from his left hand. Hackett, pounding along ahead of Mendoza, swooped for it and slowed to break it open. "Empty," he panted. "A .38— Berry! For God's sake stop! Berry!"

Just as Stass was almost up to him, Berry took a violent fall, stumbling over some hidden rock, and plunged ten feet down to a narrow gully. He lay still, sprawled grotesquely, arms and legs wide.

Hackett reached him with Stass, but Mendoza flung himself down on his knees and turned Berry over to his back. "My God, that rock," said Stass. There was a big flat boulder there beneath Berry's head; no blood, but already a wide darkening bruise on his temple.

"Berry!" said Mendoza urgently. "Berry, for God's sake can you hear me, understand me? *¡Jesús, María y José!* Berry—did you bring them here? My children—did you have them? *Por favor, Santa María*—tell me!"

Berry's face looked ravaged. His eyes opened slowly to stare into Mendoza's, dull and fixed. He said very politely to Mendoza, "I have two children, sir." And then his eyes shut and his head fell to one side.

"No, he's not dead," said Mendoza tersely to Sergeant Lake. "Massive skull fracture, nothing to say if he'll live or die. He's unconscious in the hospital at Big Bear. And it's all up in the air. Still. You don't know this country up here—"

"Yes, some," said Lake. "Pretty, but wild."

"*¡Válgame Dios*, say it twice! I don't know how long we'll be here. There's nothing in the cabin but the start of a suicide note, which is *nada absolutamente* one way or the other. But he's had three days—if—to clean it up. Anything. The Rangers are bringing in the dogs, the helicopters."

"Yes, I see," said Lake.

"You can switch me to Traffic, Jimmy. I want a chopper too."

And Lake would know what for. As he waited for Traffic to answer, Mendoza rested his head in one hand for a moment. Talk about wild country—and this whole great acreage, scrub and underbrush and a lot of tall forest, had a wry name among the lawmen roundabout: the forest of disappearing children. How many mysterious vanishings up here, even the hint of something wild, unimaginable, occult. No, he thought, no. If Johnny and Terry were up here somewhere, it was no little green men out of a spacecraft responsible. If—

He laid on the helicopter from Traffic, and called Alison. She was being very good, very quiet. She listened to him, and said, "Yes. There's no sense asking what you think. You don't know. All right, Luis. What should I give them?"

"Any clothes that haven't been washed. Toys they'd played with lately. There'll be a man from Traffic to pick it up. *Querida*, I don't know when I'll be home. I want to stay here, awhile at least."

"Yes, *amado*. It's all right, Luis. *¿Qué es esto?*" she said suddenly. "What—" And Valenti's voice snarled at Mendoza as he seized the phone.

"What the hell's going on? Have you got a lead you didn't pass on? Listen, Mendoza—"

Mendoza put down the phone.

But before that, with Palliser and Grace still out of the office, and Piggott off checking that stake-out on Fliegel's car, at ten-twenty Sergeant Reeder called Robbery-Homicide.

"Sergeant Hackett there?"

"No, sorry," said Lake.

"Well, let me talk to somebody." Lake gave him Glasser. "Listen, I don't know what your office's interest is in Andreas Koutros, but from the little Hackett said I gather you've got one."

"Yes, what about it?"

"Well, damn it, he's walked away. You know he had a job at that hospital? They called me yesterday when he didn't turn up—they know he's on P.A., of course. I went round to his room, and he's cleared out—jumped parole.

Goddamn it, I thought he was going to be a quiet one, he'd seemed to settle down—"

Glasser's pulse jumped a little. Koutros? This had looked to him all along like the tragic but common thing —was it going to turn out an offbeat one? Berry, and now Koutros. "Why didn't you let us know sooner?"

"Why should I, damn it? Oh, for God's sake, those threats on the lieutenant. Well, nobody's ambushed him, have they? I've been busy getting out a want on Koutros. Hope he hasn't got far, we'll pick him up. He hasn't got a car, and he's a loner, doesn't know anybody here, and he can't have much money on him."

"Well, thanks for letting us know," said Glasser. He sat back for a minute, feeling uneasy about this. Koutros. Art had said he was alibied for Tuesday morning. Glasser went out to Wanda's desk and asked if she remembered about that. It hadn't been an official report, of course, but if Hackett had automatically taken it down it would be in his notebook; and Wanda was concerned about this too.

"Yes," she said at once, "it was a barbershop just up from the hospital, on College Street. Why?"

"I don't know," said Glasser. "Koutros may be back in the picture." There was nobody else there to talk to about it. Matt was going on to that inquest. He went out for his car and drove up to College Street, found the barbershop a block up from the hospital. He had found an official mug shot of Koutros in Hackett's desk. He didn't waste much time on the barber, who was fat and Italian-looking with a handlebar moustache.

"Somebody was asking about this man the other day." He showed the photograph. "If he was here last Tuesday morning."

"So what?" said the barber.

"Was he?"

-155

"And what business is it of cops? You're another one, aren't you?"

"That's right." Something else occurred to Glasser. "Does he come in here often?"

"Sure, sure. Regular customer."

"Well, that's a lie. He's only been out of Folsom two weeks."

"Folsom? What the hell—"

"So how could you know him that well, to say if he was here?"

The barber stared at him. "Folsom! What'd he do?"

"Murdered his wife."

"*Dio mio!*" said the barber, and crossed himself. "Look, mister, I'm an easygoing man, live and let live, I like to oblige people. This guy, I knew him from the hospital, my sister was there last week, I seen this guy, one of the orderlies. He come in here and told me his ex-wife's making trouble, tryina grab his salary, and they'll nab him for sure, she find out he's got a girl. He asked me to say he was here last Tuesday. He give me five bucks. I like to be obliging—"

"When?" asked Glasser.

"Uh—Wednesday afternoon, late. I didn't know he was—what's he done now?"

"I don't know," said Glasser uneasily. But there it was: Koutros didn't have an alibi. On the other hand, Koutros hadn't arranged the alibi until after Hackett had talked to him, which told him the day and time he needed one for. Oh, yes?

And if this was, incredibly, the offbeat complex thing, nobody had told the Feds about Berry and Koutros.

He was still sitting there worrying when Piggott came back.

"The inquest was open and shut. Fliegel isn't going

156-

to show. That car's still there. I let the stakeout go, and told the garage to tow it in."

"Yeah," said Glasser. "And what had we better do about this, Matt?" He told him about Koutros, and Piggott looked surprised.

"You think we ought to tell the Feds?"

"I don't know what the lieutenant 'd want."

"I think they'd better hear," said Piggott slowly. "Just in case."

"Damn it, I never thought it was a planned thing, Matt, but this—it looks a little queer."

Piggott agreed with him. Reluctantly Glasser called Warren's office, and got chewed out for the information. Warren landed at the office fifteen minutes later to get chapter and verse, just as Mendoza called from Big Bear, and jumped all over them for withholding information.

The moon was still almost full.

Luis had called at nine o'clock, sounding very tired. "The dogs haven't turned up anything, and the Rangers say three days doesn't matter, they're good. I don't know —if there was any trail, you'd think it'd start from that cabin. But there's the hell of a lot of country up here, all wild. . . . Berry's still unconscious, they operated this afternoon. We've shut down the hunt for tonight, start again in the morning. I'll probably be back tomorrow. The Rangers know this country, and they're experts at trailing—we're not. We can't do any good here."

"It's silly to ask what you think about Berry. He had —the gun."

"And apparently just one full load for it. *No sé, cara.* He wasn't, maybe, very sane. Then. *¿Quién sabe?—¡Sabe Dios!*"

Alison lay awake, with the full moon streaming

through the window, going down now and around to this side of the house. She remembered so much, over just four years and a bit. Joking with Luis that it might be twins—on both sides of her family. The rather desperate time they'd had before they found Mairí. And inevitably, when the twins began to talk, not knowing English from Spanish, both she and Luis as apt to come out with one as the other. . . . All the construction camps down south of the border—a funny sort of bringing up, she supposed, Dad left with her when her mother died—

The McGuffey Readers had helped a lot in sorting out languages for the twins. And it was a little joke too, about elderly parents, Luis forty-two when they were born, but they were very bright children indeed. Only she'd never thought to try to explain—that everybody in the world wasn't good, and loving, and kind.

"*Mamacíta?* Daddy?" murmured Terry.

"Be quiet," said a low voice.

Terry woke up most of the way, to confusion and misery and loss. Once she had things come at night and Mairí said *just dreams.* But these bad things had lasted a long, long time. She couldn't remember how long—except that Johnny had been *estúpido* about the car— and the man who grabbed her so tight smelled funny —and now her dress was all dirty.

It was the same place, with the bad things still here, the bad people. She could hear them talking. Like the stories *Mamacíta* and Mairí read, the bad witches and *el lobo* eating grandmother and Rumpelstiltskin. A long time. She remembered in a misty sort of way how it started —Cedric barked and barked, and there was a gun—her daddy had a gun, a real one, not a play one like Johnny's—

And there was the lady.

Johnny. Suddenly frightened *awful,* she sat up to

look for Johnny. But he was asleep right there. He was terrible dirty, *muy sucio*, and so was she—her dress all dirty and nasty, and that made her insides feel bad. It was a long time back to Cedric barking—and Mairí and warm milk before bed and *Mamacíta* telling about the letters to make words and the kitties to pat—

In the stories bad people got dead. *La bruja* all burned up in the stove.

Terry was almost asleep again, but hurting—the floor wasn't to sleep on—and Johnny was a big *tonto imbécil*, crying all the time—

"Please try to be quiet, darling," said the lady.

The lady's name was Christine. And the story—the story in the book—said about the mama takes the little chicks under her. But Terry half woke up again and reached to touch Johnny, because the lady was nice—but she was awful scared too. Awful scared. Terry could tell.

Nine

On Friday afternoon, doggedly getting on with the leg-work to be done, Palliser and Grace had set out to find Edward Whiting. Thalia was first annoyed and then arch with them, finally parted with an address on Fountain Avenue.

"The Feds," said Grace, "are mad as hell because nobody told them about Berry or Koutros."

"Well, no real reason to before," said Palliser. "I wonder how the hunt's going up there. You know, Jase, I can *see* Berry—doing a thing like that. The way Art said he was feeling. Like a dog in the manger—if I can't have mine—. But if that's so, if they're up there somewhere in that damned wilderness, they might never be found at all."

Grace didn't say anything to that because it was un-answerable.

The place on Fountain was one of the jerry-built new garden apartments, painted orange. They got no answer at the door with Whiting's name-card in the slot, but an emaciated blonde sunning herself in a bikini in the patio told them they might find Eddy at the pool hall down on Western.

They found him there, kibitzing at a game, and he was rather interesting from their point of view. Whiting was younger than Thalia, early thirties maybe, and a little too plump and smooth, with soft white hands and an ingratiating smile and a limpidly straightforward gaze from protuberant blue eyes. He had on shabby, too-loud sports clothes. He said heartily he was always glad to help out the boys in blue, which was a warning rattle.

"Oh, about poor old Lester getting shot, damn shame that is—yeah, of course m' sister told me, always runs to little brother. Poor old Lester. But say, if you think I got any idea who did it, forget it. I don't know why anybody'd want to shoot the old, er, geezer." He told them, very open and affable, that he was a wholesale salesman of novelties—"Kind of mixing business with pleasure right now, they stock some of my stuff here—" and no, sir, he wasn't married, not him. He was sure sorry he couldn't help them out with some ideas, but it was a mystery to him—poor little Thalia all broken up, but Lester getting over it, he understood. As they turned away, his eyes went a little shrewdly speculative too soon.

"Novelties," said Grace. "Covers a wide field."

"And I would bet you," said Palliser, "that some of the money Thalia wangles from her doting husband finds its way to Whiting. It could be that Lester was beginning to balk, get his eyes open a little."

"It's funny," said Grace, "how an otherwise sensible man can be taken in by one like that, but they are time and again. But if you want my considered opinion, I doubt if Whiting has the guts to shoot anybody."

"But just at one glance, Jase, he is just the kind of small-time sharp operator, on the fringes of the law possibly, who might know a punk to hire."

"There is that," agreed Grace. And as a rule, turning this up, they'd have laid it before Mendoza, who would know all about the case: was it worthwhile to bring in Whiting, lean on him some? But Mendoza wasn't thinking about any of the cases passing through the office.

When they got back to Parker Center, Higgins had called in from Big Bear: negative results from the hunt so far.

Palliser went home, to find Roberta just tucking the baby into bed, and told her all about Berry, and the hunt with the dogs and helicopters. "But if that's how it was, we may never know. They might never be found."

Roberta looked at him, dismayed and horrified. "That's—I don't know how anybody could live with that, John. Never knowing for sure."

He didn't either. But the facts were there to face.

Mendoza called in to the office before he called Alison, to report. The night-watch men didn't feel much inclined to discuss it, though Galeano maintained that the Berry thing was too far out, while Conway thought it was the likely answer.

"What's the odds, for God's sake?" said Schenke roughly. "What you're saying is, either Berry pulled a snatch to get even with the lieutenant—for the love of God!—and most likely killed them and buried them up there, or it was a stray pervert in their own back yard, in which case they could be dead anywhere."

"Well, I suppose that's what it comes to," said Galeano sadly.

They didn't get any calls—Friday night building up to Saturday night—until nine o'clock, when they got a buzz from a Traffic man.

162-

"There's a want out on a guy named Koutros—your office and also Welfare and Rehab, for jumping P.A. We just picked him up."

"For God's sake, where?"

"Just by chance, at a brawl in a bar on Twelfth Street. After we'd picked up the drunks we just happened to notice him—we'd both seen his mug shot and once seen never forgotten. No, he's not drunk—just a few beers. You want us to call Welfare and Rehab?"

"No, no, that's O.K. Where is he?"

"Facility on Alameda."

"Of all the breaks," said Schenke. "Personally, since we found out about that alibi, I think Koutros is a damn sight likelier than Berry." He called Sergeant Reeder, and he and Conway went over to the jail to see Koutros.

He was slumped on a bench in a holding room, a heavy big dark man with a stubble of gray beard and secretive dark eyes. He looked once at Reeder and growled inarticulately. "And just what the hell do you think you've been doing?" asked Reeder disgustedly.

"I just wanted to be left the hell alone," said Koutros in a bass mumble. "Cops!"

"We've got some questions for you too," said Schenke. "Why did you try to build that fake alibi with the barber, Koutros? What were you up to instead?"

"Nothing, nothing, nothing, for Christ's sake. I get out, everything quiet and easy, first thing I know cops at me—where was I, what doing, when and where and how and why—" He lifted a big fist and brought it down on one knee. "Goddamn it, I had a bellyful of all that!"

"The alibi," said Schenke.

"Oh, Goddamn it! First I think, I slip that guy a fin to say I was there—how the hell do I know what cops think I was doing last Tuesday? And then I thought the hell with the whole thing—push a damn cart round that stinking hospital, tell this big bastard here, yes, Papa, I been a good boy—"

"You've been a damn fool," said Reeder. "You know you'll go back in now."

Koutros just growled like an angry bear. He wouldn't answer any more questions and they had to leave it at that.

"What do you think?" asked Schenke.

Conway shook his head. "He sounds level to me. Do you think he's the type to—well, take such a subtle sort of revenge, Bob?"

"Subtle!" said Schenke. "My God, I do like your choice of words, Rich. Subtle!"

"Well, but it would have been. I don't see it."

When they got back to the office, a telex had come in from Washington. That O.D. found in that hellhole last Sunday—"Yeah, I heard something about that," said Galeano with a grimace, "and too many spots like it in the inner city"—hadn't been known by his prints in L.A. records, so they'd been sent on to the Feds. He had been on record with them. He had been one Daryl Perkins, twenty-four, rap-sheets in Seattle, San Francisco, possession, B. and E., burglary. There was no record of any relatives, so the city would have to bury him. "No loss," said Conway cynically.

At ten-fifty they got another call from Traffic, and Schenke and Galeano took it. When they found the address on Elden Avenue, they had a little surprise. The average LAPD patrolman, with training and discipline behind him, is cool and efficient under any circumstance, however bloody or messy or violent it might be. But at the curb by the black-and-white, Patrolman Zimmerman was being sick in the gutter, while a visibly shaken Bill Moss was leaning on the trunk looking as if he wanted to be sick. It was an old four-story apartment building, and a crowd had collected; there were two more squad cars there, the other men herding the crowd back from a place near the side of the building. Part of the crowd were evidently tenants from the apartment, all of them talking excitedly.

An ambulance was catered in behind the first squad car, lights flashing, and inside it a man was screaming hoarsely, wordlessly. Another ambulance came up and attendants got out of it. It was hot and breathless in this narrow old street.

"You said there wasn't a hurry. D.O.A.?"

"Oh, my God," said Zimmerman.

"What's up?" asked Galeano. The first ambulance purred off and the screaming mercifully died.

Moss gestured up toward the side of the building. "He threw them both out the window. The two kids. From the top floor. He's high as a kite on something."

"Oh, Jesus," said Galeano.

"We don't know where the mother is. The neighbors say she works nights, but don't know where—they hadn't lived here long. Kid about three, and a baby."

"Sweet Mother of God!" said Galeano, and went to look. They were both dead, very bloodily dead.

"There's Mis' Calero now—" a single loud female voice from the crowd on the steps. They turned. A woman was walking up the block from the bus-stop on the corner. Seeing the crowd, the squad cars, the lights, she began to run. They got her as quickly as possible in the back of one of the squad cars; they might need another ambulance for her; they didn't want her to see the bodies.

But she just stared at them blindly at first, Galeano talking quietly, Schenke twisted around in the front seat.

She was a young woman, shabbily dressed in a shapeless blue uniform, a young woman who looked very tired, with great dark eyes like an Italian madonna.

"They're dead?" she said blankly. "My baby Ricky and Maria? He—"

"We don't know what he'd been taking, Mrs. Calero. Does he get to drinking often?"

She shook her head slowly. "He don't drink," she said dully. "He'd 've got hold of some speed or something. Anything. I try to keep money away from him. I—try—so—hard. But he'd always get hold of something. Somehow." And then she began to cry, and they called up another ambulance.

"Dear heaven, what we see on this job," said Schenke. But the two small broken bodies had just reminded them all over again of the hunt up in the mountains. Probably shut down for the night now, to start up again at first light.

"I've heard those Rangers' dogs are good," said Galeano, following the unspoken thought.

"Let's hope so. At least that poor woman knows where her children are now," said Schenke somberly.

At six o'clock on Friday evening Mr. George Lonsdale, of Lonsdale Realty in Beverly Hills, had been feeling restless. It wasn't an evening to sit home and watch TV, he told his wife Elaine. He'd just concluded a pretty big deal which was going to put a sizable piece of money in his pocket, and he felt like celebrating. As a responsible citizen, Mr. Lonsdale wasn't one to go out and tie one on, but he liked a cheerful evening at a genial place, with a few drinks and a good combo to listen to. His wife enjoyed an evening out too; they were sociable people with a good many friends, substantially well-off people in their late forties, and with their two daughters conveniently married and off their hands they felt pleasantly irresponsible these days.

So Mrs. Lonsdale put on her newest cocktail dress—a white sheath, for she had been lucky enough to keep her figure—with pearls, and Mr. Lonsdale shaved again and donned his newest sports jacket—brown plaid, with brown slacks—and they got into their air-conditioned Cadillac and drove up the Malibu highway to the Trancas Beach Inn, a favorite place of theirs. Mr. Lonsdale had two double Scotch-and-waters, and then the lobster and steak plate, and Mrs. Lonsdale had two vodka gimlets and (conscious of her figure) the special chef's salad. They ran into several couples they knew, and the combo was good; they had a pleasant evening.

At ten-fifty they came out to the car. It had cooled off a good deal by now, with the Pacific washing the sand just across the highway, and they didn't turn on the air conditioning. Mr. Lonsdale had had another drink after dinner, but he was nowhere near tight and he drove sensibly as he always did, at a steady forty-five in the middle lane. They had just passed the entrance to Topanga Canyon, on their way home, when an old sedan came burning rubber with a screech like a siren out of that road, just missed a VW in the left lane behind the Cadillac, and hit the Cadillac broadside like a bomb. The Cadillac, thrown into the right lane, barely nicked a Ford Mustang on its way, turned over, burst into flames and went over the palisades onto the beach. The sedan came to a smoking stop on its side.

As luck had it, Sheriff's Deputies Pete Sharpe and Andy Lane were half a mile up the highway. When they came on the scene two minutes later Sharpe said, "Jesus!" and piled out to look for corpses, while Lane called up some help.

There were four people wandering around the sedan,

two couples, the beards marking the males. They weren't hurt aside from minor scratches, and they were laughing and shouting and pointing gleefully at the burning car. They were all high on something, not liquor.

"My good God in heaven," said Sharpe when the fire was out and two charred bodies had been taken away, "it's just like the old days with the drunks, never hurt themselves, only the other people!"

The two men sat quietly on the back porch of the house. It was very hot tonight here in the inland valley.

"Shame your little vacation had to turn out this way, Fred."

"Just one of those things. We had a few good days anyway." The other man dropped a hand to the head of the dog beside him. "I'm just glad Bob's going to be all right."

They'd meant to make the camping trip last a week, but on Wednesday the boy had been taken so sick, with a high fever, they'd rushed him back to a hospital. There'd been an emergency appendectomy yesterday, and he was getting along fine.

"Anyway you can stay on till Sunday—if you don't mind the weather."

"Hot down in the city too. I'll try to get Christine in a little while. She wouldn't expect to hear from me till tomorrow night."

Christine half knelt, half lay against the door of the tiny cramped closet. The fetid hot air seemed to sear her lungs. Her mind was sometimes quite clear and then all fuzzy again, and she didn't know what day it was; time had stopped meaning anything.

The curious thing was, she thought dreamily, that at the beginning it had seemed absurd, melodramatic, even a little funny. Such an ordinary morning it had been.

Been having an orgy of reading since Fred left: must have been her first time out of the house, except to empty wastebaskets. There'd been a letter from Fred Junior.

The children. Somebody's children. Who? Polite children, nice. Long time since she'd had a child to worry about.

A gun. In her own yard, on a summer morning. Those two. Cheap bravado. It had been absurd.

And then not.

The little boy stirred and she reached lethargically to him, on the floor beside her. He was very hot, probably had a fever. It was unbearably hot everywhere, but in here—and if he cried—

It wouldn't matter. All the other noise.

Her head was aching damnably. Those two. The big one with the gun, the beard. The other one with the wet mouth and nervous little giggle. It had turned to nightmare when they came to this place—nameless, filthy, noisy place—she didn't know where. She still thinking, absurd, lots of people around, scream, get away— He had hit her with the gun, there had been a car—and then dark stairs, feeling of people around, smells— *She's a li'l high, 's all*— and this place, one squalid little room, reeking bathroom.

Tried to tell. Not there. Wouldn't be there. The big one angry, hitting her again. At first she tried to tell them too, about the children. Not hers. Somebody else's. But it was so queer—it was as if they used words of English, slurred and flavored with the same obscenities over and over, but didn't understand it. No, didn't listen. Not bothering to listen. The big one shaking the little girl, *where's your old man*—not listening, not understanding.

My name's Teresa Maria Mendoza. Frightened, thin little voice—that was all in English. Didn't know anybody named Mendoza. Who?

Then thinking, keep quiet. If they knew the children no use to them—something terrible? Because that was after—after—when the two men had gone away, and the children were hungry. Banged on the bathroom. door a long while—please, something to eat for the children— and when the door opened, the men gone. Please, she had begged. They were girls. Other females. Then the nightmare darkening, as she looked at them—really the first time.

The utter indifference in shallow eyes. The complete unawareness of her, the children, as other people. The emotionless mild curiosity of a young savage. *That was what they were,* she had thought suddenly then.

And so hard to talk to them—shout through the eternal, senseless, ear-blasting thump and clash of the radio, the primitive jungle beat—savage, savages, young savages—

She's been askin' for something to eat. Much later? *Oh, hell, we got no bread buy stuff, dammit. . . .* A hamburger, greasy onions, cheese, wrapped in dirty paper. The little boy had been sick.

The big one dragging her out. From the reeking bathroom, closet? Words flung at her. The gun, and hitting her again—her jaw felt stiff and sore. Docile then, she tried to tell him what he asked: deep in nightmare, her head ringing from the blows, the tormenting beat of the too-loud radio, she told him.

Try to keep the children quiet. This place so hot. Noise—once, traffic outside, dim?—but the radio forever beating against the unbearable heat—

Fred wouldn't be back until Sunday. No one to miss her.

The children—whose?—seen before?—where?

Then, awhile later, suddenly her mind clear again, and she heard them talking out there. The radio suddenly still. Arguing. The words—arguing about bread, that was money, the language they used. Money in the bank, she thought, and she remembered banging on the door again, desperate, to get their attention, and then somehow make them understand. *I can give you money, I've got money to give you.*

A mistake. That had been a very bad mistake. They had understood, finally. The shallow eyes eager, greedy, the rank unwashed smell of them close around her. Stupid—she had to tell them what to do. The two men back, arms full of miscellany—they must have ransacked the house— *My God, I left the house open for any burglar—* Her jewel case, clothes, Fred's clothes— *Gotta lot o' stuff we can hock, man.* The checkbook. Didn't remember the balance. Too big, they'd question it. What kind of money was big to these incredibly stupid, powerful young savages? The check—

A bad mistake. Because that was when—nightmare again, and all she could think, surrealist—nothing real, nothing sane. *Got us some meth and good grass, man—* Jungle scene. Jungle—obscene couple on the bed—noise—the radio again, and not to let the children see—

Drunk and incapable, her mind had said. Get away while they— But her head hurting so, and one of the girls screaming, the big one coming—

There was something heavy against the door of this little closet, she couldn't move it. Her head seemed to be expanding slowly like a balloon. It was hard to breathe—so hot, too hot.

Outside the door, the radio blared the endless beat, thump and clash of cymbal and drum. Jungle music.

The little girl muttered, *"Mamacita?"* Christine put a fumbling hand on her: fever. And the air—how long would the air last in a tiny place like this?

Her mind blurred again and went away.

On Saturday morning, before the day shift came on, a stolid Japanese hailed a black-and-white cruising down Fifth Street. "Dead man," he announced to the patrolmen.

It was indeed a dead man, hidden behind some tall oleander shrubs in front of the public library. Apparently he had been shot; there was a lot of blood, but not new; the corpse was very cold. The Traffic men called an ambulance and talked to the Japanese, who was the gardener at the library. He hadn't been there for a week, he sai until today.

That was waiting at Robbery-Homicide when they all came in, and some paperwork had to be started on it. Sergeant Lake was off, Farrell sitting on the switchboard. Farrell got moved around, sitting in for men in different offices, but he'd heard all the grapevine could tell, and Grace was bringing him up to date. Yesterday, the day before, as the news passed about the big building, they'd had others calling in—some of the men who had worked with Mendoza over the years, Captain Callaghan and Lieutenant Goldberg of Narco, Lieutenant Andrews of Vice—Sergeant Barth up in Hollywood.

Glasser went over to the morgue and looked at the dead man. He didn't need to have a hunch about it; the corpse rang loud bells in his head. He asked the only doctor around to send any slug over to the lab, and went on to that twenty-four-hour café near the Stack. Halloran wasn't there but he got the address in Walnut Park, and routed Halloran out to come back to the morgue.

"Well, I'll be damned, that's him, far as I can tell," said Halloran. "The heist-man. My God, did I kill him?"

"That's what it looks like, Mr. Halloran. He ran out, you said, didn't seem to be hit bad—but it looks as if he took a slug in the stomach. Got up there a block and a half, and some instinct to hide maybe, not thinking he was hit bad, got in behind those bushes and bled to death. Not surprising nobody spotted him in twenty-four hours."

"I will be damned," said Halloran. "Say, that don't make me feel too good, killing somebody. Even a heist-man. God, he looks young. What—what do you do now?"

"Well, we'll have to borrow your gun to test-fire some slugs for comparison with the one from the body. Just checking. There'll be a hearing—next week sometime probably—but it'll get called justifiable homicide, you don't need to worry about it."

"Well, my God, I do worry about it," said Halloran. "Me, killing somebody. I'm sorry about it, but it was his idea to hold me up. Who was he?"

"We'll hope to find out," said Glasser. When he got back to the office Hackett and Higgins were there, and Mendoza was wandering around smoking. There was a Fed still sitting in his office, and he was annoyed about that. He looked almost his usual self—he'd been home, Glasser deduced, for a shower and clothes, and was sharp-dressed as always, a darker gray suit than usual—but he looked thinner, taut, and very tired.

"Those damn zealous Feds are annoying the Rangers," he said sardonically as Glasser sat down. "Insisting on joining the hunt. A bunch of city men. The Rangers know what they're doing."

"But if they haven't—found any trail up to now," said Palliser, "is it likely they will? The dogs—"

"Lot of country up there," said Hackett. "If there's anything to find, it could be anywhere. It could be days—" His voice trailed off. It could be never.

"If Berry wakes up halfway sane," said Higgins, "we could find out right then."

"That's what we'll hope, George."

"What about Koutros?" asked Grace after a silence. Conway had left a note.

"¿Y eso qué importa?" said Mendoza. "I don't know."

"Luis, I wish you'd go home to bed," said Hackett. "We'll let you know the second anything breaks."

"I'm all right, Arturo."

-173

"Well, that's a lie," said Higgins bluntly. "And no wonder. Go home, Luis."

"Maybe later. I'm all right," repeated Mendoza mechanically. The phone shrilled on Hackett's desk and Mendoza picked it up before anyone else could reach it. "Yes, Rory. Big Bear, yes. . . . Oh? Oh. . . . Yes, thanks very much for letting us know. Yes, too bad. Thanks." He put the phone down very gently. "Berry died an hour ago without regaining consciousness."

Hackett let out his breath in a gusty sigh. "So that's that."

"That's that," said Mendoza, and put out his cigarette. He picked up the perennial black homburg, and his hand was shaking just a trifle.

"Luis—it's still all up in the air. We don't know a damned thing. Anything could happen. Have happened. We don't—" It was a fairly desperate effort. Mendoza gave Higgins a twisted one-sided smile.

"Five days," he said. "Five days since Tuesday morning." He went out, and left silence behind him for a long minute.

Then Higgins said, loud and violent, "Goddamn it! Goddamn this whole bloody world for the Goddamn things like this!"

"Now you'll juist please me by getting this down." Mairí stood over Alison with a cup of bouillon. "And don't tell me you're not wanting it—that I know—but whatever it may please God to send us, we've got to look at the facts, *achara*. And the fact is—" her face twisted momentarily— "if you havena anything else left, you've got your man to look after."

"Yes, Mairí."

"And you needna be telling me either how long it's

174

been. All things possible with God, *mo croidhe*, and He's been good to answer my prayers before now."

"Yes," said Alison.

"Yon man!" said Mairí with a snort. The FBI men sitting on the phone had become collectively *Yon Man*. "Nothing whatever he's doing to earn his keep, and it goes against my heart having to feed him. You get that down and mind what I'm saying."

"Yes," said Alison. Five days, she thought numbly. She had got past any impulse to have hysterics or even cry. She wondered if Angel, or Mary Higgins, thought she was unnatural. Things didn't seem very real any more. Time first slowed down and then speeded up. Five days. But some innermost part of herself was screaming soundlessly, *Where are they?*

It wasn't the big new one in Hollywood with its white tower and imposing steps in front. It was the one he had known—a very long time ago. The squat little one, humble and square, almost the first building in what had sprawled into this vast complex of city jungle. He remembered his grandmother bringing him here, she in her shabby black dress and dowdy black hat. Always just the two of them, his parents dead in an accident before he was a month born. The old man an angry old bear of a miser, grudging every penny. And Luis Rodolfo Vicente Mendoza just another Mex kid running the streets down here, the narrow old slum streets—turning a dime where he could. Nobody knowing about all the loot the old miser had accumulated—doubtless some of it by way of the stacked decks and crooked hands. Not until he was an idealistic rookie riding a black-and-white on patrol, and *imbécil* enough to stay on that thankless job.

Teresa Maria Sanchez y Mendoza, ramrod straight

and a cunning contriver of excuses to worm another dollar out of the old man—but she hadn't managed to get him a new suit for graduation from sixth grade; all the rest of them had new suits, but it hadn't mattered so much because she told him how proud she was, he the tallest boy there and the best marks. . . . And such a shameless liar she was too—all the grand Castilian ancestors.

The place had suddenly so vividly conjured up a long list of memories that Mendoza felt confused: this time, another time? Time did not mean very much to this place.

He had had a paper route. Never told her why he could give her the five, six, seven bucks a week, on top of the two from the paper route: errands for people, and she said he was a good smart boy. Set up a Spanish Monte bank in the back of Johnny Li-Chong's father's restaurant —he had always been good at handling the cards. But she disapproved of gambling: go the same sinner's way as the old man.

He took off his hat and went in. Well, she had lived to enjoy the old sinner's loot. Such childish pleasure she'd taken, the expensive apartment, and buying all the shrewd portable value, the diamonds, the emeralds—

Maybe more of both of the old ones in Luis Rodolfo Vicente Mendoza than he'd ever thought.

The look and smell and feel of the place sharpened everything in him, and he thought remotely what an old place it was. It had seen much of the good and bad in life, and remained forever aloof, committed but unchanged.

He went slowly up the aisle. There was nobody here: nothing but the single flame answering briefly to unseen currents but serenely alive.

The old remembered things came back haltingly. He had to fumble for the words, the old words, and it was right they should not come back to him in the English.

"Dios te salve, María, llena eres de gracia, el Señor es contigo, bendita eres, entre todas las mujeres, y bendita sea el fruto de tu vientra, Jesús. Santa María, madre de Dios, ruega, Señora, por nosotros los pecadores ahora y en la hora de nuestra muerte."

The flame seemed to tilt, as if politely, toward him.

"It is," said Landers, "hot."

"I won't argue with you," said Phil. "Cooler here."

"A nice beach down there," said Landers. "And this looks like a fairly good motel. Air-conditioned."

"So?" said Phil.

They had got away from Fresno at noon, and cut across to the coast road. It had been hot in the inland valley, but here at the coast it was better. They had stopped here outside Guadalupe for an early dinner.

"Well, there's bound to be a hell of a lot of traffic the rest of the way down, on a Sunday," said Landers. "It doesn't really matter whether we get back Sunday or Monday. What would you say to staying here overnight and maybe relax on that beach tomorrow? There's a sign about some caverns to explore."

"I'd love it," said Phil. "I can't say I much care when we get back to the rat race."

"There's a vacancy sign. I'll go and register."

------------------------ Ten

Palliser and Grace were alone in the office at ten minutes of twelve, and Palliser was just about to suggest they go up to the cafeteria when Sergeant Farrell looked in.

"Kind of a shy pigeon on the phone," he said. "Said ordinarily she wouldn't go across the street to help out cops, but Linda was a pal of hers. She's been off on a little trip, just heard about Linda getting took off. She says you might look for a character named Jackie May, said to be a regular customer of a disco house on Vermont, the Blue Neon. Linda'd been making it with him lately."

"That's interesting," said Palliser. "I thought Linda was going into Pending." Neither of them moved to start doing anything about Jackie May. The disco house wouldn't be open now. Grace said lackadaisically that they'd better run the name through R. and I., see if he showed in records.

At about noon on Saturday, a bored Sheriff's Deputy, Bill Carney, was trying to clear up some details on that accident on the Malibu road last night. The four people left alive had all been doped up, and brought in to Central Receiving; hopefully, today they could at least tell their names. But when Carney faced the two males, a small bell sounded in his head, and he called in to his own office and then Robbery-Homicide.

"That artist's sketch you were circulating. I think we've found a match for it, right here. Have you got some witnesses handy?"

Palliser said regretfully, no, they were back in Merced; but that sounded interesting, and he and Grace went to look. The shaggily-bearded, still vague-eyed young man looked a lot closer to the sketch than that Podmore had.

The old sedan had been towed in to the police garage in Santa Monica; nobody had looked at it very closely as yet. When they did, they found a lot of clothes bearing name-tags marked *Goodman,* an expensive tool-chest labeled *James Goodman,* and several knives of various sizes.

"This looks like a jackpot on that Merced murder," Palliser told the sheriff's boys. "Who are these dopies?" They hadn't got names from any of them, but at least they had them, with some good evidence.

They sent a telex up to Pomeroy about it. Tomorrow, or next day, the dopies might be back to whatever sane senses they had, and could be questioned, the inevitable paperwork started. But all of that would be Pomeroy's job, and the arraignment and trial up north.

A mistake, she had thought that. To let them know she could give them money—any kind of money. Don't again—the jungle noise, the jungle scene— She tried to say *No,* but her tongue didn't move—pain— Then her eyes focused sharp for just one second, and frighteningly she wanted to laugh, she wanted to cry with laughing—for he had her checkbook in his hand, pushing it at her, open, and she saw there were no blank checks left in it at all, just the little account pages at the back.

Please, she said soundlessly. Didn't they understand, if they killed her she'd be no use to them, to get more money? Fred—

The children—

Then he hit her again, and dark came down.

Hackett had been on the phone to Big Bear when the call came through; Higgins took it. "This is Verna Fliegel," said a cool voice. "You asked me to call if he showed up here—Joel. He did, this morning. He's broke, and I've got him convinced to talk to you and turn himself in." She sounded a little cynically amused. "He says he might as well get three squares a day in the joint as starve to death outside."

Higgins didn't smile. "Thanks very much, Mrs. Fliegel. I'll come and get him." He didn't bother to tell anybody where he was going; he'd be back soon enough.

In the comfortably shabby apartment, he found Verna Fliegel, neat and smart in navy blue, watching her ex-husband wolfing a ham sandwich. "Made me late for work," she greeted Higgins dryly. "I've been all morning persuading him to turn state's evidence, if that's what you call it."

"Listen, I don't want to rat on anybody," said Fliegel. He was a middle-sized man about forty, good-looking if he'd had a shave and a better haircut, and decent clothes.

"They've already got one of your pals," said Higgins. What the hell had the name been?—he dredged it up with an effort. "Rodney—Roderick Pratt."

"Oh." Fliegel finished the sandwich, looked annoyed, and then shrugged. "Oh, well, then. Nobody got anything off that caper, Sergeant, and I wouldn't care one damn about putting that—that *kid* on the spot. That *kid!* I tell you, it's been a lesson to me, it sure as hell has." He was indignant. "I'm not denying I've got a rap-sheet, or Pratt either, but we also got some sense, I hope. You set out to do a job, you use some sense at it, not so? But that kid—! Pratt was two minds about bringing him in on it, but we needed another man—"

"For the hostage?" said Higgins.

Fliegel just shrugged again. "Neither of us ever tried that big-time a job before, but I guess it'd have gone O.K. except for the kid. Letting go the loot nearly as soon as he got hold of it, forget all we told him about drop a decoy—damn fool kid been smoking pot or something, I found out afterward."

"You can tell it to the boys in Sacramento," said Higgins, bored. "Come on."

Fliegel stood up. "Brother," he said, "any time I pick up with a kid again—! That one, I got to know him at a flophouse up there, he's a big strong kid, calls himself Thor—God, what a name—thought he'd be useful, see what I mean, but these kids, they've just got no sense of responsibility, what it comes to! Of course the other one tagged after him all the time, he's no more than a piece of wet rag on Tuesday morning. But that Thor—"

"Tell it to Sacramento," said Higgins. As he took Fliegel out, the woman stood watching with inscrutable eyes.

"Looks like you kind of blew it, Thor darling," said Su-Su. "Like maybe she's out for keeps." She pushed her hair back, staring at the woman on the floor. "I guess she is. I can't see her breathe."

"Oh, hell," said Thor.

"What do we do if she is, huh?" Ollie's compulsive giggle was strained.

"You want I should lay out the cards and see what

they say to do?" Tally was divorced from the little group around the woman; she sat cross-legged on the bed, shuffling the dog-eared old Tarot deck. They were all used to talking over the sound of the incessant radio.

Thor said what she should do with the cards.

"The kids are asleep or something," said Su-Su. It had been a long time since she'd been Susan Briggs with a nice, permissive, country-club set of parents and a neat suburban home and anything she wanted to ask for. Twice she hadn't run far enough and they'd brought her back, so the next time she ran far and wide and she'd been running ever since. With different people; without people. But she kind of liked Thor, he was big and tough like a guy ought to be.

"What'd we do?" Ollie giggled again. He'd never been much at all until he took up with Thor. The orphanage, kicked around because he wasn't bright.

"You still got the kids," said Tally, still busy with the cards, indifferent. "That guy'll pay to get his kids back." Tally didn't think much of any of the people or any of the life she'd seen so far. Crazy lushy mother named her for some silly actress—school people telling her what to do and she got out of that—drifting around easy, ever since, she didn't remember when it started—the sex bit she didn't go for but if you had enough barbs or speed it didn't matter, and days blurred into days. She'd been thinking just today, get enough bread somehow, like off by herself, set up some place and tell people's fortunes with the cards, a fun thing, and nobody around after the people went away. Good.

Thor just looked at the woman. He never said much, and they didn't know much about him. He came, and was. He said, "And how the hell we gonna tell him? He's not here. She hadda know where he is, she wouldn't tell!"

"Well, I'm not going to stay here with a dead body," said Tally. "It's too hot."

"Oh, hell," said Thor.

"The kids don't look so good," said Su-Su. "But that guy'll want 'em back, all right. When *he* comes back, see? We can get out of here, who'd know the old bat was hooked up to us? Wait till he comes back. Like, a real snatch. Get some real loot, way we set it up at first."

"I'll lay out the cards," said Tally. "She must've been real old, fifty maybe, that's the Queen of Wands—"

The Robbery-Homicide office was very quiet at ten minutes of two that afternoon. There hadn't been any calls in a while; Sergeant Farrell was reading a paperback. Hackett was the only one there, and that was mostly from inertia. He was just sitting there, his mind a gloomy sort of blank, when Farrell buzzed him and said the hospital had just called. Lester Mordway was conscious and very anxious to talk to the police.

"Mordway?" said Hackett. "Oh, yes." The little man shot at the bank. Palliser's rather offbeat case. He got up heavily; the habit of discipline was strong in him, and the tiresome routine had to be done, whatever happened in private lives. He said, "All right, I'll take it."

At the hospital, a bright-eyed pink-cheeked nurse in a white pantsuit was waiting for him, and hurried him up to a two-bed room where a screen stood shielding the bed nearest the door.

"Are you police?" gasped the man there. He was a middle-aged man, going a little bald, and there was thick gray stubble on his jaw. "Police?"

"Now don't try to move around, take it easy—" The nurse fussed.

"Yes, I'm police. Sergeant Hackett."

"Got to tell you," said Mordway weakly. "Don't know —how long been unconscious. So—so surprised—but got to tell. I—"

"Who shot you, sir? You know?"

"No—doesn't matter—but they said—listen, Sergeant, they said—holding Mr. Orrin's wife and children—hostage. Wanted money—from the bank, before—let them go. They—"

"What?" said Hackett.

"Mr. Orrin—bank manager—not here. On vacation. So they said—I could get money—instead. Two—young—louts," panted Mordway, sounding stronger. "Louts. Didn't mean to shoot me—a crazy thing—heard one say, It just went off. Didn't mean—but you've got—find out— —about Mrs. Orrin. But—"

"For God's sake," said Hackett. He thought rapidly, Wednesday—get the address, find out where Orrin was, at the bank.

"But—the Orrins don't have any children. Queer," muttered Mordway. "Grown-up son. Don't know—if the louts meant—in the house. You've got to find out—don't know how long—it's Laurelton Place—"

"Laurelton—" said Hackett, and then he said in a great voice that made the nurse jump, *"Laurelton Place!"* and he bolted for the corridor. "A phone—where's a phone—"

When he braked the Barracuda in front of the house on Rayo Grande Avenue thirty minutes later, he was late on the scene. Palliser's Rambler came up the drive behind him and Palliser and Grace got out of it. The front door was open; they pounded down the hall past the big living room, Mendoza's den, through the kitchen and back door and down the big yard. Cats fled, and Cedric was barking loudly down there by the wall.

Over the wall was the alley, and everybody was over there in the next yard. They piled over two walls to join them.

"Right here?" Alison was saying. "Right *here?* They had climbed the wall a few times, but we—"

" 'Twas the puppies here then." Mrs. MacTaggart was excited. "You mind they told about the puppies—"

Mendoza appeared at the back door with Valenti behind him. "The place has been ransacked," he said. "All wide open. Warren's talking to the bank."

"But how the hell—they must have been here when the—the louts came," said Hackett. "But why—"

"Deductions a little superfluous, Arturo," said Mendoza, "but we can make some. She was out in the yard —Mrs. Orrin. Maybe Johnny and Terry thought there were more puppies, anyway they'd climbed the wall and were here too. When the would-be bank-heisters came on the scene. What did Mordway say?—young louts. Mmh, yes— took it that they were the Orrins'. And—"

"But they couldn't still think that, Luis!" said Alison.

"We don't know the ins and outs, *cara*—but now we've got some idea of what happened, at least."

"Five days!" said Alison.

"We've got to find Orrin," said Mendoza. Hackett and the others followed him into the Orrin house. Warren was on the phone in the hall. It must have been a neat and handsome house once, deep-piled beige carpet, solidly furnished bedrooms, bright cheerful kitchen, a lot of books in the living room; but it had been turned upside down, ransacked ruthlessly and at random, drawers pulled out and dumped, clothes pulled from the closets.

"All right!" said Warren. "He's been up in Stockton visiting his brother—they're out on a camping trip, but somebody'll know where—get the police up there—the phone number ought to be here somewhere—"

Mendoza had already found the phone-index. "Here it is. It may take a while to locate him, let's get on it for God's sake!"

But Fred Orrin was ten feet from the phone up there, because of Bob's appendix.

Christine wasn't all the way back, but dimly aware of something different. Not nearly as much noise. She lay there for a long time thinking muzzily about that, before she got her eyes open. Her head was like a balloon, she'd never had such a headache in her life—couldn't remember how she'd got here, where she was—dirty floor, clothes filthy— *Young savages.*

No radio. Gone? Cautiously she tried to move, to look. She thought, there had been some children. Nobody, now. Noise, nearby, but different.

Traffic. Brakes—engine noise.

Get away now. Try.

She ached all over, she couldn't get up, there was pain like fire in her side, but she crawled, panting, blind, got the wrong door—the closet—crawled again, and there were voices. It was *Them* again—

Hey, old bag's really doped up. Couldn't see clear, but dirty jeans, leather jacket—girl in a bikini, long hair—loud coarse laughter. Please help me, she tried to say it. Then she fell headlong down a lot of stairs, and the laughter rose to braying senseless noise.

Hell, let the pigs pick her up, man. Throw her out.

Traffic noise close. What felt like sidewalk under her hands—cement gritty, dirty. A squeal of brakes somewhere near. And then dark again.

"Do you understand, Mr. Orrin?" Mendoza had got the phone away from Warren.

"I've got you," said Orrin equably. He sounded like a hardheaded sensible man, a strong baritone voice, and he was quick on the uptake. He hadn't wasted much time on exclamations. "My God, Tuesday," was all he added now. "I tried to call Christine last night but I wasn't surprised when I didn't get her. She's got her own car. Now —I'll get down as fast as I can. May have to charter a plane at Stockton, but it's a short flight. Where do you want me first?"

"Right here, Mr. Orrin. You can give us some idea what's missing—if they've pawned any of it, that might be our first lead. Get here as fast as you can."

"I'll be there," said Orrin, and hung up.

Alison and Mairí, Palliser and Grace, were still out in the yard. Cedric was barking excitedly. There were people out in the next yard now—an elderly couple, peering over the picket fence, curious and alarmed.

"Something wrong at the Orrins' place?" asked the man. "What's up? Who are all these people?" They were being good neighbors.

Palliser flashed the badge. "There's been a burglary."

"You don't say! We never heard a thing! That's terrible, but the way crime's up these days— And both of 'em gone, too. What a—"

"You said you saw them go," said Alison suddenly. "Both of them? Last—a week ago Friday."

"Yes, that's right," said the woman. "Off on vacation somewhere."

"Do they have a dog, ma'am?" asked Grace.

"Why, yes," said the man. "Yes. A Labrador retriever, it is, it had some puppies a few months ago—valuable dog, I guess."

The woman, shortsighted, seeing the dog in the front seat? Not seeing Mrs. Orrin afterward—and that was coincidence.

Fred Orrin got there at five o'clock. He was a rather handsome man about forty-five, not tall but stocky and wide-shouldered, with a cap of dark hair and steady, shrewd dark eyes. His eyes flicked over the ravaged living room, and he acknowledged the brief introductions with a nod. "You've been on this five days—and the FBI. I'm sorry about the children," he added gravely to Alison. "Nobody's fault, but I'm sorry." And to Mendoza, "Tell me what you want me to do." Within half an hour he'd given them a good idea of what was missing; Hackett went to get that hunt started, but it would take time.

"I don't understand how you can get any idea," he said to Mendoza. "Where would they take her—them? How do you look?"

Mendoza was looking keyed-up, excited, if still very tired. He had been chain-smoking all afternoon. "We don't have any idea, Mr. Orrin. But we know now they've been, mmhh, frustrated for some time. First they found you weren't at the bank, after they'd taken their hostages. Then we can deduce they thought somebody else there might be persuaded to pay the ransom instead, and approached Mordway—"

"How would they know who—"

"Names on doors, Mr. Orrin. At the bank. John—" he swung on Palliser—"how did that go? You were on Mordway."

"Jase and me. Wild-goose chase," said Palliser succinctly. "Thalia and little brother. The heisters knew Mordway's name, likely from a look inside the bank. Tuesday afternoon? But they couldn't get at him, or didn't try, until the bank opened on Wednesday morning. And he was late—he'd just come up to the door, the guard said his name, so they accosted him right there and then."

"And shot him by accident?" said Orrin. "They're not just so efficient, are they?"

"¡Cómo no!" said Mendoza. "And so that frustrated them further—Mordway wasn't in any condition to get the ransom for them. What have they been doing since?" He flicked his lighter.

"What indeed?" said Orrin, and his voice wasn't raised but there was a snap in it. "Are you telling me, what you just guessed about these bastards, taking the wrong hostages—or two wrong ones—before finding out I as the mark wasn't even here—and then accidentally shooting Mordway who was supposed to get the money instead, if you're reading that right—are you telling me you think there's any remote chance that my wife and your children are still alive? After five days?"

"There's a chance, Orrin. We've got to play it as if there was a chance," said Mendoza sharply. "So they sound like amateurs. That makes it a better chance. They'll still want the ransom, if at all possible."

"How do we play any hand at all?" asked Orrin.

Mendoza opened his mouth, and Warren appeared in the doorway looking sourly amused. He flung an open newspaper into Mendoza's lap.

"For once the press is working for us," he said. "Mordway's nurse talked. Loud and clear. Getting in on the act."

"*¡Vaya por Dios!—¡no me tome el palo!* The luck runs our way, friend!"

"What? What's happened?" asked Orrin.

Mendoza unfolded the first section. "Lefthand column front page—and *buena suerte* to you! Oh, very nice indeed—*¡me gusta!*" The headline read, *Bank Manager's Wife Hostage to Kidnappers—Ransom Demand Expected.* "We couldn't have asked for anything better."

"Luis—" Alison came to lay an uncertain hand on his shoulder. "Will they see it? Where *would* they have been keeping—all of them? I can't imagine—"

"Easy, *cara.* One step at a time. With more luck, we'll know."

Orrin had taken the paper. "Publicity," he said. "So this says I'm here, I know, I'd pay the ransom. Do you think it'll draw them?"

"There's a good chance. The Feds are already busy out there—" as Orrin twisted his head— "transferring the tap from my phone to yours. We'll now contact all the radio and TV stations in the area and get them to broadcast an appeal, with your phone number—on the hour every hour. We—"

"This doesn't say anything about the children not being mine."

"*Gracias* for small favors. The nurse didn't catch that bit, maybe. You are prostrated with worry," said Mendoza, "and very anxious to hear from the kidnappers—willing to pay any ransom to get the family back safe—"

"Am I?" said Orrin. "Yes. I'd have to arrange with the bank—Saturday night, but the board of directors—"

"*No hay tal,*" said Mendoza. "Unless they ask for half a million, leave the ransom to me. And we sit back and wait."

"And *wait,*" said Orrin. "Five days! And the damned idiotic way these—amateurs have been acting, we suppose they've still got the hostages, safe and sound—"

"*¡Despacio!*" said Mendoza, and his eyes were cold and his voice like ice. "I don't know, Orrin, and you don't know. That's the chance we take. But I'll put it to you like this. If you don't happen to draw a royal flush, wouldn't you settle for a Dutch straight? If you missed the jackpot, would you settle for table stakes?" He came upright from where he'd leaned in the chair, and his eyes held Orrin's. "If that's so, what's in your mind, *hermano,* don't you want a chance to nail them? If we can?"

"Yes. I get you there. Yes," said Orrin. "All right, whatever you say."

Alison couldn't stop shaking. It was silly, now they

knew something, now it wasn't just a great big blank. Now there might be, just might be, a chance. It was a hot night, close and muggy, but she felt cold, and she couldn't stop shaking.

It was a good melodramatic story, and radio and TV seized on it gladly; it was broadcast regularly into the night. At the ravaged house on Laurelton Place, they sat and waited. Every hour the appeal went out: *grief-stricken husband pleads with kidnappers to call him.* The number repeated.

They waited. It was a long night. Mendoza sent Alison and Mairí home. Palliser and Grace went away, and Hackett came back to sit with the rest of them.

But Su-Su usually left the transistor radio at the all-music station. It was eleven o'clock the next morning, when she was fidgeting with the dial and heard the tail-end of the renewed appeal.

"Hey," she said. "Hey, Thor, it's about this guy—it's for us!" She spent a while getting that into his head. "Maybe they'll play it again."

An hour later they did.

"He says, any ransom, get them back. We can still make it! Tally, you write down the phone like I said to?"

"I got it."

"We ain't got the old lady no more," said Ollie.

"Damn stupid," said Su-Su. "He doesn't know that. We can call and tell him where to put the money—fifty G's, we said that much when we started."

"Where?" said Thor. "There's no good place, safe. They spot cops all around, wherever you pick."

Su-Su bounced on the seat. "*I know a place!*" she said excitedly. "Listen, Thor! That place we had the blow-out —up the coast—it had a funny name. Sauquit Point!

There's a sign. And it's like the end of the world, nobody and nothing all round—you could see any cops a mile away! We'll tell him to put it right by that sign, and no cops—no helicopters either, the cops use those, it shows them on TV. We just go and pick it up, no sweat."

Thor and Ollie looked at her with grudging admiration. "That could be pretty damn safe—empty as hell there, it sure was," said Thor slowly.

"What you gonna do with the kids?" asked Tally. They were sitting in the car, parked by the curb on a narrow residential street in Hollywood, eating hamburgers. The kids were huddled supinely on the floor of the back seat.

"We've gotta keep them till after," said Thor. "You make the call, Su-Su. And one thing you're gonna say, and say it good—" He paused. "I better make the call. They wouldn't believe a chick. We tell them, anything goes wrong, any cops or choppers like you said, they all get killed. Right then. They get their throats cut. Only, if everything's O.K., nice and easy, we—oh, we let them out ahead somewheres."

"How long would it take to get up there?"

"Hell, I dunno. Hundred and fifty miles maybe. We'll need some gas for the heap. How much bread we got?"

"Well, tell him like nine tomorrow morning. That'll give us time get there."

"But we ain't got the dame now," said Ollie. "Just the kids."

"Shut up, stupid! The guy'll pay just as much for the kids!"

The voice was strong, tough and young: just that hint of uncertainty that made Mendoza's nose twitch. His pulse quickened a little as they listened to the tape recording for the tenth time, there in the Orrins' living room. He

192-

didn't say what was in his mind. He'd dealt with the wrong ones a long time; and the hardened, experienced old pro, however coldblooded, didn't as a rule go off half-cocked—it was the uncertain amateurs who did that.

"Sauquit Point," said Warren. "You got it, Joe?"

"Wouldn't show on anything but a local map," said Valenti. The Feds were always efficient; they had local maps. "I got it. It's just a little bit down from Gaviota, there's an old side road leads up to the coast highway, and that's about where any sign will be."

"Set up a command post at Gaviota," said Warren, galvanized into action.

Orrin didn't move, looking at Mendoza. "You're going to play this straight? Do like the man said, no cops, no choppers around? Don't chase them or they'll kill everybody?"

"You'll have to trust the pros, Orrin," said Mendoza. "We'll be up there before dark. There'll be vantage points. No, of course we don't stand by and watch them take off with the ransom. We'll have telescopes on the car, get the plate-number, roadblocks all ready to set up whichever direction they take."

"Do you believe they'll have my wife and your kids in the car?"

Mendoza regarded his cigarette. "No," he said deliberately. "I should doubt it. If they're still holding them, they'll be left somewhere. Maybe with accomplices—it's in the cards only a couple of them will come to pick up the ransom. But when we drop on them—"

"When is the hell of a long word sometimes, Lieutenant," said Orrin. "I can't say I place so damn much faith in your reading a license plate through a telescope, and I've driven that coast road—there are a hundred side roads off it, and you won't have a hundred roadblocks ready to roll out at a word."

"We play the hand we've got," said Mendoza harshly, "the best way we know how. . . . By God, I thought that once, this was deuces wild, and hasn't it been all the way!"

Orrin laughed. "But in that game, Lieutenant, the joker's wild too."

"Anywhere in the pack," said Mendoza, and met his eyes. "Are you coming?"

"Oh, yes, I'm coming," said Orrin. "I've got my wife's car, thanks. Have you got the money?" He didn't seem to be interested in how a police lieutenant could lay hands on fifty G's in cash at short notice.

"I've got it. And if we're going to get up there by dark—¡Vamos!"

"You know I'll call you just as soon as we know anything, cara."

"Yes, Luis. Good luck," she said tremulously. "We'll be—holding good thoughts, amado."

"I'll be praying hard on it until you fetch them through that door!" said Mairí fiercely. "And so you will be—I know in my soul you will!"

It was cooler, that much farther north. Gaviota, which was just a truck-stop and a café on a bare lonely hill, had been thrown into excitement by the advent of the Feds. Warren had commandeered the little second-story room which afforded tourists a breathtaking view over the Pacific, as his command post. He and the other Feds had set up a battery of communications with the Highway Patrol, the Coast Guard.

Mendoza and Hackett had got up there at five-thirty on Sunday afternoon, in the Ferrari, and sat up most of the night drinking black coffee in the little café, with the Feds coming and going on various errands. They had gone out to look at the sign before dark.

At five-thirty in the morning, among these lonely rising hills and dipping hollows, this place was as bleak as the mountains of the moon. "The land God forgot," Hackett muttered, shielding his lighter from a cold dawn breeze. But Mendoza was fidgeting and nervous. "Orrin," he said. "Damn it, Art, Orrin! He said he was coming. Where the hell is he? I don't trust that man."

A lonely, lonely place, not the hint of any farm building, even a fence, anywhere around. But hidden away here was quite a crowd of waiting men, unseen, unheard. Mendoza and Hackett were lying flat just below the gentle crest of a hill overlooking that road: an old two-lane blacktop road leading toward the coast. They could see the sign from here, a stark arm raising a single board. *Sauquit Point Rte. 101 1 mile.* Mendoza swept his field-glasses around a circle from that, not bothering to focus on the limp briefcase at the base of the signpost, dropped there before dawn and watched from first light. Beyond, across from them here, another great swelling hill rose, swept down to a hollow westward, and he could see a vague worn track—footpath, bridle trail—at its bottom. Up to another rise of hill, and a higher one behind, a few red-and-white cattle grazing there. This side, more rolling sweeps, sparsely covered now, the summer grass browning. But also here, this high, he could see over the crests beyond to the glint of blue-green Pacific a mile, two miles west. And below them here, on a rude trail wandering in from that road down there, were two FBI sedans, radios, walkie-talkies. Beyond the next crest, two more cars. More men across the road, hidden behind hilltops, waiting and watching. Up the coast, down the coast, the Highway Patrol alerted.

And what the hell use would it all be? he thought sudden and savage. Settle for table stakes! Nail them and punish them? And even that you couldn't be sure of, these days: he thought about Arnold Berry.

A hand touched his ankle: one of the Feds, crawling

up. "Something coming through for you on shortwave, Lieutenant."

All Mendoza's nerves quivered alert. Something found? Something— He handed the glasses to Hackett and slid backward down the hill, across rough scrub grass. In one of the black sedans below, the shortwave radio crackled at him, and carried the distorted voice of Sergeant Barth.

"—Mrs. Orrin!" it said. "We've got her—she was picked up last night on the street, in front of a fleabag rooming house just below the Strip. She just regained consciousness and told us who she is. You getting this?"

"Sé—how is she?"

"She's been beaten up, ribs broken, a cracked jaw and concussion, but she'll be O.K. But that's all she came out with, just her name, before she passed out again. I've got a man standing by in case she comes to again any time soon—"

"Yes. *Gracias.* Good news." The luck, thought Mendoza, the luck! Superstition! But he'd always been lucky.

He crawled back up the hill. They waited. The sun rose higher, and nothing stirred in all this lonely bare land. His watch crept slowly on to nine o'clock, nine-ten, nine-twenty.

"Wait for it," muttered Hackett, and lowered the glasses. And down there on the empty side road, there came cautiously around a curve from the inland side an old sedan. An old white Dodge, battered and filthy, slowing at the signpost. Stopping.

He snatched at the glasses, tried to focus them sharper—too far down, too acute an angle, he couldn't see into the car. Somebody on the passenger's side slid out, fumbled on the ground, got back in. The Dodge began to move again.

And right now all the Feds would be feverishly busy,

on the radios, on the walkie-talkies, efficiently getting the roadblocks alerted—soon enough? How many side roads to take, they could slide out of pursuit in five minutes, the damn Feds always so sure of themselves, but a thousand things could go wrong with this Goddamned setup—

The Dodge picked up sudden speed down there, rocketing around a curve to the west. And then, as he lowered the glasses, Mendoza saw the second car. It came with a roar, motor wide open, out from its hiding place in the fold of hills where that bridle trail wound down. An old pale-blue T-bird, making tracks over the short grass, bouncing onto the blacktop after the Dodge—

"*¡Diez millones demonios*—Orrin!" he shouted savagely, and flung himself down the hill toward the Ferrari. "That Goddamned idiot Orrin—"

The Dodge screamed around the last curve onto the wide coast highway. The T-bird was holding on, a hundred yards behind.

Thor was driving, accelerator on the floor, eyes wildly swerving to the rear-view mirror. "Ollie!" he yelled. "Ollie—Do it! Throw them out—throw the kids out! We said—if there was any cops, any—" The Dodge was doing ninety-six in the middle of the road.

The cold fresh air with its tang of salt had revived Terry to half awareness. She opened her eyes dully as hands grabbed her by the body and lifted her. Car—going awful fast it was—rush of wind on her face—*where was Johnny?*—the bad people, the bad man who smelled funny, holding her tight—

She twisted her head down and bit his hand as hard as she could, and he yelled, *muy ruidoso*—

They had made a leisurely late start down the coast; it was a beautiful morning, cool and golden, with the sun sparkling on the tranquil summer Pacific. There was practically no traffic on the highway at all; they'd be back in L.A. by afternoon.

"Back to the rat race," said Phil with a sigh.

And Landers had just added idly to that, "I wonder what's been going on down there," when there was a siren some way ahead, and he slowed. There was a wide hairpin bend coming up.

Around it, motor wide open and snarling, burst an old sedan on the wrong side of the road. Landers stood on the brake. The sedan hit the Gremlin's right front wheel a glancing, shuddering blow, just enough to deflect it off course, and was thrown violently onto the west shoulder of the road, ploughed through sand and shale and stopped, teetering over the edge of the drop, smoking.

"God!" said Landers. They got out shakily.

Both rear doors of the sedan had sprung open. One small body had been thrown clear, lay limp back from the edge.

Phil ran. She saw another child—a little girl, halfway out of the glassless rear window. She reached up and caught her by both shoulders and pulled her out over the trunk, just as the car rocked for the last time and went over, two hundred feet to the rocks below, with a dull crash.

"*Tom—*"

"He seems to be O.K., no bones broken—"

But their voices were drowned in the siren, cutting off like a throat slashed, the roar of engines. The T-bird slithered to a stop screechingly, the Ferrari cut in behind it, three cars behind. Men were running, shouting.

"*Lieutenant!*" said Phil and Landers together, astonished.

But the little girl let out a squeal of joy and wriggled from Phil's grasp. "*¡Aquí me tienes,* Daddy! The bad man was gonna throw me 'n' Johnny out of the car, but I bited him hard!"

"*¡Gracias a Dios—gracias a María— ¡Mas vale tarde qué nunca!*" Mendoza had her tight, and took Johnny from Landers in the other arm. On rather shaky legs he went to the edge of the drop and looked over. He said, to the idle tide washing over the pile of junk down there, "*¡En paz!* So we call it quits!"

They got identification for three of them, with a little trouble. Nobody was going to miss them much. There wasn't much left of the green paper in the briefcase.

The one who called himself Thor they never identified. He came out of the dark, went into the dark.

And on the succeeding Sunday morning, Alison and Mairí were fondly superintending the twins' breakfast at seven o'clock. The cats had been fed and were sunning themselves in the back yard, undeterred as usual at this season ("I do wonder what happened to the creature," said Mairí) by the audacious mocking bird. Cedric was hanging around hopefully after bacon or anything else available.

The twins were squabbling amiably over the last piece of toast. "It's a great mercy," said Mairí, "how verra resilient children can be, *mo croidhe*. The dear wee lambs."

"It's a word for it," said Alison, "thank heaven. Well, you are early, Luis." She regarded Mendoza in some surprise as he appeared at the door to the kitchen, dapper in silver-gray Italian silk, snowy shirt, dark tie. "So you're back to concentrating on the thankless job, *mi marido honorable?*"

"Not," said Mendoza, "for another hour." He clapped on the homburg and turned to the back door. "I am going to early Mass, and I'll hear no—mmh—extraneous comments about it."

They were both still staring after him open-mouthed when the Ferrari's engine faded down the driveway.

DATE DUE